A Family of Violence

Jon Athan

D1520889

For more information on this book or the
author, please visit www,jon-athan.com. General
inquiries are welcome.

Facebook:
https://www.facebook.com/AuthorJonAthan
Twitter: @Jonny_Athan
Email: info@jon-athan.com

Cover designed by **Sig**:
www.inkubusdesign.com

ISBN-13: 978-1546699606
ISBN-10: 1546699600

Thank you for the support!

WARNING

This book contains scenes of intense violence and unpleasant themes. Some parts of this book may be considered violent, cruel, disturbing, or unusual. Many of these scenes include a young teenager. Certain implications in this book may also trigger strong emotional responses. This book is *not* intended for those easily offended or appalled. Please enjoy at your own discretion.

Table of Contents

Chapter One

A Haunted House

"I swear, the house is haunted. I've heard it from five, maybe six people already. You can hear a ghost screaming in there. A girl ghost, you know? She screams, then she runs at you. They say she tries to grab you 'cause she lost her kids or something. It's crazy, man," Richie Adams said.

Richie planted his palm on a moldering tree trunk, then he stepped over a muddy puddle. He left an imprint of his black-and-white sneakers in the mud with each calculated step. He moved slowly, trying his best to avoid an embarrassing tumble. Traversing the dreary woodland was difficult considering the recent rainfall, but he was able to persevere.

Trailing behind him, Stanley King said, "Yeah, yeah... You think we'll get there soon? It's getting late and I have to get back home before it gets dark. My dad will be pissed if I'm late again. You know how he gets."

"I know, man. It's right around the corner. Besides, we still have an hour or two. It's not going to get dark right now. Relax, man, take it easy."

Stanley huffed at Richie's nonchalant demeanor. Richie, a close friend, was not going to get in trouble for running late. It was easy to dismiss Stanley's concern when it was not one of Richie's problems.

Should the sun fall within the hour, Richie would emerge unscathed and Stanley would fade into his bedroom – a never-ending grounding.

Richie was a naturally blasé young man – 13 years old, to be exact. He was a chubby teenager. His dome was covered with curly brown hair, like if a filthy mop were sprawled across his head. He wore a red windbreaker jacket and blue jeans. He didn't care for fashion or popularity. He was a free spirit, pursuing his interests on a whim.

Richie turned towards Stanley with his index finger on his lips – *shh!* He whispered, "Do you hear that?"

Stanley slowly shook his head and said, "Nope."

Richie glanced towards his left, Stanley followed his lead. Before another word could be uttered, a neighboring bush rustled. The shrub swayed and crepitated like if it were hit by a flurry of wind. The pair stared at the bush, pondering the reason behind the motion. *Can a ghost leave the house?*–Stanley thought. The idea seemed preposterous, but a bush moving without a draft seemed uncanny.

Richie coughed to clear his throat, then he asked, "Is someone back there?"

A squirrel darted out of the bush and hurtled towards Stanley and Richie. The pair stepped aside and watched as the squirrel scampered away. The woodland critter sought shelter in a dying woodland – a hole in the ground or a bush with leaves. The prying couple couldn't help but chuckle at their fear. A squirrel was nothing to fret over.

As he stared at the furry critter with deviant eyes,

Stanley asked, "Do you want to kill it?"

Richie furrowed his brow and tilted his head. Astonished by the question, he asked, "*What?*" Stanley continued to stare at the squirrel as he deviously smirked. Richie snapped his fingers and asked, "What did you just say, Stan?"

Stanley blinked erratically as he snapped out of his unusual trance. He stared at Richie with a raised brow, baffled. He could not force himself to admit it, but he actually couldn't remember what he said. As far as he knew, he did not utter a word. He remembered the squirrel, but he could not remember his words.

Stanley shrugged and said, "Nothing, nothing..."

Richie narrowed his eyes as he examined his friend – *his best friend.* Stanley was the same age as Richie – at least for a moment longer. He was an introverted teenager, still growing accustomed to his skin. He was lean and tall, consequently moving with an awkward hunch. He didn't want to draw attention to himself, he did not want to stand out in the crowds.

Stanley's resplendent brown hair was combed over to the right, feathery and wispy. His dark brown eyes were indecipherable. Duplicity and deviance occasionally sparked in his pupils. He wore a black jacket over a white t-shirt. His black jeans and black sneakers were muddied by the pair's trek. Like his friend, he did not care for his appearance or popularity.

Richie shrugged off the violent offer. He said, "Well, we should check out this house before it gets dark. I don't want you to get in trouble. I know you won't stop complaining if you do. Come on."

As Richie walked ahead, Stanley jogged to catch up. Walking side-by-side, the pair strolled through the desolate woodland. Richie dug his hands into his pockets and kicked at rocks and clumps of dirt on the ground. Stanley hit the passing bushes with a large branch. The couple were searching for any activity to lighten the mood.

Richie asked, "You excited for your birthday party?"

Stanley smiled and responded, "*Adventure Planet?* Yeah, man, I'm excited. You're coming with us, right? Your mom already let you go?"

"Yeah. I was going to go anyway. She says 'no,' but she really means 'yes.' At least, that's what I *think* she means. You know how it is."

Stanley nervously smiled and said, "Yeah... I'm just worried about having to go back to school the next day. You know Mark and his punk friends are going to try to hit me or... or, I don't know, they're going to try something. I know it."

"Don't worry about those punks, man. They're a bunch of little bitches. They only want to fight if they're together. Besides, you ride the Shriek-and-Creak with me and I'll handle those guys for you. I'll take care of those punks. I've been teaching myself how to box. I think I can knock them out with a few punches. Yeah, I can do it..."

As Richie shadowboxed, Stanley glanced at his friend and nodded. The compromise was bittersweet. On one hand, Richie would offer a sense of security to him; on the other hand, he would have to ride a thrilling roller coaster. Although he had some strange tendencies, like the occasional suggestion of violence, he was not very fond of fear. Yet, in the back of his mind, he knew Richie would protect him anyway – roller coaster or not.

Stanley sighed, then he asked, "Are we almost there? It feels like we've–"

Richie interrupted, "*We're here.*"

Richie stumbled over a bush, barely keeping his balance. The thick foliage was tangled around his feet. Stanley jumped over the shrub, avoiding the mess. The pair stared at the secluded house in the woods, awed by the discovery. The house was a local legend, a cautionary fable told to bad children. *Don't go into the woods, there's a haunted house out there!*

As he gazed at the house, Stanley said, "Wow. It's... It's bigger than I thought."

The white two-story house was surrounded by towering trees. The dilapidated house was hidden due to the overgrown area. Although visible at a close range, the house could not be spotted from afar. The shrubs, the foliage, and the trees veiled the legendary home. The planks of wood on the exterior were chipped and every window was shattered.

Richie said, "Alright, let's get in there. You have your phone? I want to record something. Get some proof, you know?" Stanley did not respond. He stared at the house, paralyzed by the lingering dread. Richie gently shoved him and said, "Come on, man. Don't bitch out now. We didn't walk all the way out here for nothing. Let's go."

Stanley glanced at Richie and sighed. He wanted to drop everything and run home. Yet, he knew he'd be deemed a coward and he knew Richie would not let him live it down. He was in a lose-lose situation, so he opted for the less demeaning option.

Stanley sighed, then he said, "Okay, let's go..."

***

The hinges squealed as the door slowly swung open. The splintered front door opened up to an entrance hall. There were three doors below the staircase to the right. To the left, an archway led to the living room. A vile miasma wafted through the hallway, pummeling any vulnerable nostrils with an odious stench.

Richie held his jacket to his nose and said, "Damn, it smells like crap in here. Smells worse than my toilet after we had Mexican food. You remember that?"

Holding his shirt to his nose, Stanley nodded and said, "Yeah, it was *my* toilet."

"Oh, yeah. It was your toilet, wasn't it? It doesn't matter. It smells bad in here. Even with the broken windows, this place smells like crap. I wonder what it is. Dead animals or something?"

"I don't know and I don't care. Why don't we just go home? Huh? We'll leave the door open and let it air out, you know? Let's come back some other time. This is too gross."

Richie huffed, then he said, "No. If we leave now, I know you'll never come back here. I know you, man. Just follow my lead. Let's check this place out for a few minutes."

Richie walked into the living room, glancing around the unfurnished area. There was only a single couch towards the center, directly across a sooty fireplace. The couch was ripped to shreds, the original color was unidentifiable – puke green, perhaps. The floorboards groaned with each step, like if the ground would collapse due to their weight.

Stanley muttered, "We always do this stupid shit... Damn it..."

Stanley reluctantly followed his persistent friend. He was repulsed by the trash lingering on the floor. Rotten food wrappers, contaminated syringes, and used condoms clung to the floor like lint in a wallet. Yet, he was not sure if the garbage was the source of the stench. As he walked through the next archway, Stanley found himself in the kitchen.

Richie opened the refrigerator, then he gagged. He looked away and said, "Holy shit, man. This place is sick..." He held his forearm to his nose and walked away. In a muffled tone, he said, "It's like someone's been living here. Shit, man, this might be some sort of hobo hideout."

Stanley stood on his tiptoes and peeked into the fridge. To his utter surprise, the broken refrigerator was stocked with food – meat, milk, and juice. The food was rotten, but it was stocked nonetheless. Richie's theory seemed to have some weight. *A nest for hobos,* Stanley thought, *I have a bad feeling about this.*

Richie glanced up at the ceiling. He asked, "You want to check out the second floor or should we head home? I don't hear any ghosts around here.

Must have been a bunch of lies..."

Stanley said, "We should just go home. I've probably got less than an hour to run back to my place. I don't know if your mom cares, but my dad does. I told you we were wasting our time."

"I don't know. I thought it would be pretty cool. I swear, Jennifer, from math, she said she was up here with Isaac and they heard a woman screaming. They said it was a ghost, but it was probably some bum. They're so stupid."

"Let's just–"

A bloodcurdling shriek disrupted the friendly chatter. The feminine screeching echoed through the home, reverberating through the lonely woodland. The ghastly scream was filled with agony. The awed pair glanced at the floor. The racket clearly came from below.

Wide-eyed, Richie said, "*The basement.*"

Richie stumbled back into the main hall. He glanced at the three doors, eagerly searching for the correct answer like if he were on a game show – *what's behind door number one?* He was hurtling towards the horror, sprinting towards potential danger. Although reckless and dangerous, he was not going to pass up on the opportunity to see a ghost.

As he rushed to his side, Stanley said, "Let's go. Come on, let's get the hell out of here."

Richie stared at the first door in the hall with inquisitive eyes. He shook his head and said, "No, no, no. *Hell no.* We can't just leave. We could find something here, man. We can become legends. Get your phone out and start recording."

"*No.* None of that matters, Richie. There could be someone in here. It could be a bum waiting to throw shit at us or something. Let's go."

"Don't be such a–"

A ghoulish groan interrupted the argument. Once again, the moan was filled with pain, raspy and long. The pair stared at the door directly ahead, shocked. The scream seeped from the crack beneath the door, calling to the couple – a call for help. Of course, Richie was willing to answer.

Richie grabbed the doorknob and said, "I'm checking it out. Just have your phone ready in case you have to call the cops. It's that simple."

Stanley rubbed the nape of his neck and said, "I don't know about that. It's not that simple. It's *never* that simple."

Disregarding Stanley's concerns, Richie opened the door. He stared down the rickety stairs with a furrowed brow. Due to the ominous darkness, the stairs appeared to be endless – a staircase to hell. Richie swallowed the lump in his throat, then he descended into uncertainty. Stanley shook his head as he watched his foolish friend. As much as he hated his carelessness, he couldn't allow Richie to enter the basement by himself.

Stanley pulled out his touchscreen cellphone and muttered, "It better be worth it, Richie..." The stair howled like a wolf to the moon as he took his first step down. As he reluctantly proceeded, Stanley whispered, "It better be worth it, asshole."

Chapter Two

A Family of Violence

The basement was unusually cold, frigid like a snowy plain. The eerie ambiance amplified the sensation of the cold temperature. Stanley and Richie could see each quivering breath as they shivered. The couple found themselves frozen by fear. Their minds told them to run and shout, but their bodies were locked in place – fight-or-flight was a tricky phenomenon.

The friends could see the basement in all of its bloody glory. The makeshift dungeon was splattered with dried droplets of blood. The grimy gray brick walls and cracked concrete flooring were the canvases for a splatter artist with a love for crimson paints. Chains and shackles were connected to the walls. Deadly home improvement tools – hammers, screwdrivers, and coping saws – were littered on the ground.

From the bottom of the steps, the frightened friends could see the source of the screaming at the opposite end of the room. A man stood to the left and a woman stood to the right – Edward and Katina. A grunting brunette woman was sprawled across a hardwood table in front of them. Her unclad body was riddled with lacerations.

With a quivering lip, Stanley stuttered, "I–I–I... We... We weren't..."

The young teen was struck with apprehension as he gazed into Edward's sharp brown eyes. The man had resplendent grizzled hair, long and slick. His thick, unkempt beard covered his throat – a bush of hair on his face. He wore a white tank top, revealing his lean physique. In cursive, a tattoo on his chest read: *Carnage.* The man appeared mean, his scowl fueled by an uncontrollable hatred. He had a malevolent aura.

To Stanley's utter dismay, Katina smirked and twirled her long black hair as she gazed at him. She had a kittenish demeanor, winking and licking her lips. Regardless of age, she was naturally flirtatious around males. She could not help herself. The deviant sensation was hardwired into her brain. Her mind ran amok with aberrant ideas.

The young woman wore a low-cut white shirt, showing plenty of cleavage. Her blue jeans were spattered with blood. Although she was not tattooed, she had a bizarre scar on the left side of her face. The marking ran horizontally across her cheekbone with several stray lines, like a black centipede crawling on her face.

Edward tilted his head and said, "Well, it looks like we've got ourselves some visitors, darling. They don't look like pigs. No, they're far too young and they're not squealing. They look like... They look like kids that just fucked up. I mean, they really *fucked* up."

As Edward chuckled, Katina said, "Oh, I don't think so. I mean, maybe they're looking for something to fuck, but I don't think they 'fucked up.'

I *might* be happy to oblige, at least for one of them..."

"Of course you are. That's nothing new."

As the sinister couple shared a chuckle, the woman on the table whispered, "Help... Help me... Please..."

Katina smiled and said, "I'll be happy to help you, sweetie. It's my pleasure to help the *weak* and *pathetic*. I have to contribute to society somehow, right? Well, let me make my 'heartfelt' contribution now."

Katina grinned from ear-to-ear as she grabbed a framing hammer from the table. She examined the hammer with inquisitive eyes, like if she had never seen the common tool before. As she stared at the petrified teens, smirking and giggling, she nonchalantly struck the woman's dome. Each hit was stronger than the last, each thud echoed through the basement.

The victim's legs violently trembled as she went into shock. Blood jetted from a gash on her forehead. Yet, Katina did not stop the violent beating. She was not bothered by the senseless savagery of her actions. She showered in the warm blood squirting from the wound. She was relishing in her moment of ferocity. The woman was wicked and proud – a horrifying combination.

Edward grabbed Katina's wrist and said, "That's enough, doll. Let her pass with a bit of pain. Don't make it easy for her."

Katina placed the hammer on the table and said, "You're right, you're right. I lost myself for a moment. I'm just so... I'm so excited to have some boys around! This just doesn't happen very often. It's amazing!"

"Yeah, I understand that. Just keep your damn paws to yourself. You understand me?" Edward asked. Katina licked her lips as she leered at Stanley. Edward grabbed her chin and turned her head towards him, then he sternly repeated, "*You understand me?*"

"Of course."

Wide-eyed, Richie screamed – a blurt of noise. He couldn't conjure a simple word, so an indistinct shout sufficed. He stumbled over the stairs, tipping over his muddied footprints. Edward shook his head as he rushed towards the boy. He inhaled deeply as he lifted the chubby teenager from the ground. Kicking and screaming, Edward lugged Richie towards the center of the room. Richie's flailing and yelling was fruitless.

Stanley tumbled to his buttocks, then he crawled towards the wall behind him. The cellphone slipped and slid from his hands as he struggled to compose himself. He thought about calling the police, but the numbers quickly became muddled in his mind – *911, 191, or 119?* Before he could dial the first number, Katina yanked the phone from his hands, then she smashed the device on the ground. She grabbed Stanley's wrist and pulled him deeper into the dungeon.

With Richie in his arms, Edward said, "Oh, oh, oh. You fucked up, boys. We were going to let you leave, we were going to let you walk away. Why would you try to run? Huh? Why would you do something so stupid? Now we know we can't trust you. Trying to run, trying to call for help. We've got to put you to sleep, you hear me?"

Teary-eyed, Richie pleaded, "No, please, don't hurt us! We won't tell anyone, I swear! Please!"

"It's too late for that, you stupid piece of crap! You fucked up!"

As she gently caressed Stanley's cheek, Katina said, "They fucked up, I know. I want to spare this one, though. There's something about him." She simpered like a conniving child, then she said, "I want to touch him, but I don't want to hurt him. No, I can't hurt this young man. I just can't do it. I'm sorry."

Stanley trembled uncontrollably as he sobbed. His nose and cheeks were blushed. He could have shouted for help, but he did not want to aggravate the problem. The entire situation was Richie's fault. At the very least, he hoped to save himself by remaining quiet and cooperative. Richie was on his own.

With his hand over Richie's mouth, Edward asked, "You want to spare that boy? You want to let him walk out of this house?"

Katina nodded and said, "Yeah."

"I don't know about that. We have a good thing going here. I don't want to mess that up by letting this boy run around with our secrets. It won't do us no good if he talks."

"I want to let him live. There's something about him. I can see it in his eyes. Please, I don't want to hurt him."

Edward glanced at Stanley, then he stared at Richie. He said, "Well, I think we can work something out..."

***

Edward dragged Richie towards the sturdy table. Richie whimpered as he approached the slaughtered woman. He had seen death and gore through the internet and movies, but he had never witnessed real violence before. A schoolyard tussle was nothing compared to the bloody slaughter in the dungeon. Edward grabbed a large chef knife, then he tossed it on the ground in front of Stanley.

Edward said, "Pick it up. Don't try anything funny, boy, we're giving you an opportunity here. We're giving you the chance of a lifetime. Now, *pick it up.*"

Stanley wheezed as he reluctantly grabbed the knife. His hands trembled uncontrollably as he pointed the blade away from his body. The everyday kitchen knife was daunting – a common home appliance had metamorphosed into a tool of torture.

Katina gently grabbed Stanley's wrists and said, "Hold it steady, sweetie. You don't want to cut yourself with this. If you cut one of your soft fingers off, the best we can do for you is glue it back on. I don't think you want that."

As the woman giggled, Stanley stuttered, "Wha– What do you want from me?"

Edward pulled Richie closer to Stanley, then he said, "Well, to be blunt, I want you to kill your friend. I want you to stab him. Not once, not twice... I want you to stab him over and *over.* I want you to make him squeal like the pig he is. And, when you're finished, you can walk away. It's that simple, really."

Leaning closer to Stanley's ear, Katina whispered, "Do it, sweetie. Cut him up, then walk away. I'll make sure no one hurts you. You can trust me. I promise."

Teary-eyed, Stanley stepped in reverse and said, "I... I can't. He's my friend." He gazed into Katina's eyes and said, "Please, don't make me do this. I won't tell anyone, I promise. I've never... I've never snitched before. I can keep a secret."

Katina smiled and pinched his cheek, like a mother teasing her child. She said, "Sweetie, you're a big boy. You can do this. It's very easy. You just hold the knife up, then you thrust it into him. Poke through the fat a few times until he dies from the pain and the loss of blood. The blade is sharp, hun, you can even just walk into him and it'll cut him..."

Richie shouted, "Don't listen to her! They're lying to you, Stanley! They'll kill you anyway and you know it! Run! Just run!" He jerked and squirmed, trying to escape from Edward's powerful grip to no avail. Richie barked, "Run, you fucking idiot! Run! Or... Or kill him! *Kill them!*"

Edward smacked the loud teenager upside the head – one swift slap to the back of the dome like if he were swatting a pesky fly. Richie yelped from the hit, then he sobbed. His words became a garble of noise. Stanley stared at his friend with narrowed eyes. He wanted to feel sympathy, but the pity did not emerge. Instead, he felt offended. *'Idiot,'* he thought, *who the hell does he think he is calling me an 'idiot?'*

Edward sternly said, "Listen up, boy. You either

kill your friend here or we kill both of you. I've got a busy schedule, so I'm going to give you thirty seconds to make a damn choice. Now, I don't have a watch and I'm a fast counter, so keep that in mind. Your time starts now."

Thirty seconds to choose between life and death, thirty seconds to contemplate a lifetime of friendship. Under the circumstances, thirty seconds felt like an eternity. The world was whisked away as time slowed to a crawl. Stanley stood in an empty abyss, lost in his thoughts. 'Thirty seconds' and 'idiot' continued to echo through his mind.

Katina whispered, "Kill him."

Stanley tightly shut his eyes and inhaled deeply. He held the knife away from his body, then he hurtled forward. He stopped as he hit a soft body, penetrating the skin of a fluffy person with the stainless steel knife. He stepped in reverse, pulling the blade out of the mush, then he lunged forward. Two stabbings were not enough, though. He grunted and groaned as he blindly stabbed his friend three more times.

As he felt a liquid dripping on his hands, Stanley opened his eyes and gasped. His hands were drenched in blood. A few droplets fell on the sleeves of his jacket. The droplets were negligible, but he could see them – he was stained by murder. The knife was jammed between Richie's ribs, even after Stanley released the handle.

From over Stanley's shoulder, Katina said, "Good boy..."

Stanley staggered in reverse as he stared into

Richie's eyes. He could see the life fading from his body. His breathing was slow and heavy. His eyelids flickered and his head swayed. Edward held his hand to Richie's mouth, stopping him from screaming. He wanted to hear the boy squeal, but he figured a silent death would be best. He didn't know if another group of teens were exploring upstairs. The risk was not worth taking.

As Richie passed away, Edward carefully dropped him to the floor. He said, "We don't want to bruise the meat. A boy like this can offer us plenty of food for a few weeks if we store him correctly. Yeah, he seems like a nice catch. Let's just hope he's not too fat."

Katina said, "I think he'll be fine. A little fat never hurt anyone." She seductively sucked on her thumb, then she wiped a droplet of blood from Stanley's face. She smirked and asked, "Want to join us for dinner?"

Stanley slowly shook his head, astonished. The suggestion was heinous – *cannibalism*. Richie's body would be used to feed a couple of cannibals hiding in the woodland. The simple thought made him think of a horror story. Despite the horrific situation, he didn't scream. He stood with a steady posture, waiting for permission to leave.

As he browsed through Richie's pockets, Edward said, "We would love to have you for dinner, boy, but I'm afraid you're not ready for this *premium* meat. Shit, I don't think you want to feast on your friend anyway, right?" Stanley did not respond. Edward glanced back with a furrowed brow and asked,

"*Right?*"

Stanley nodded and whispered, "Right..."

"I thought so. But, shit, if you'd like to join us sometime, I think we can welcome you back. You seem like the type to hang around us without running your mouth. That's good. That's *very* good. I've always liked that about people like you."

As she rubbed Stanley's shoulder, Katina said, "Yeah. You seem like the good type. Listen, sweetie, my name is Katina. You can call me 'Kat.' With a 'K,' okay? It's what all of my friends call me. Well, at least the living ones."

Edward said, "The name's Edward. Edward, Eddie, Ed... it never really mattered. Personally, I prefer 'Ed.' It's simple, you know? You call me that from now on. None of that 'Edward' bullshit. It's too formal, too professional."

Katina said, "Start calling me 'Kat,' sweetie. It'll make us feel closer. Trust me."

Stanley examined the violent couple as they watched him. He was anxious, but he didn't fear the pair. He was feeling a medley of emotions, but fear and guilt were not at the top of his list. In an instant, Ed and Kat seemed welcoming to him. *Ed and Kat, nicknames for friends,* he thought, *are they really my friends?*

Stanley responded, "My... My name is Stanley. It's nice to..." He shut his eyes and inhaled deeply, trying to keep his composure. Stanley said, "It's nice to meet you, Ed and Kat."

Ed smiled and said, "Well, you can go home now. Just remember one thing: you have blood on your hands. You can't tell anyone about this or you'll go to prison for a *long* time. Believe me, boy, you don't want to go to prison. You don't know what they'll do to you in there. You don't know what the system will do to you. Go on. Get out of here."

Stanley nodded as he stared at Richie's lifeless body. He swallowed the lump in his throat, like swallowing a can of tuna. He kept his eyes on his murdered friend as he walked towards the staircase. The whole situation felt illusory, like if he were living through a nightmare. At heart, however, he knew he was awake.

As Stanley walked up the creaky steps, Kat winked and said, "You can come visit us any time, sweetie. I'll be waiting for you..."

Chapter Three

Home Sweet Home

The dazzling sun was setting beyond the horizon. The sky was painted with every tint of orange, creating a vibrant portrait of natural beauty. Teens and kids ran through the cul-de-sac, enjoying the sunshine before darkness reigned supreme. The children were blissfully unaware of the savagery in the woods.

Stanley only wished he could have remained as oblivious as his peers. He shambled up the decomposed granite walkway, dragging his feet towards the two-story house. He wasn't running late, but he could not wash his terrible actions from his mind. He was different and his family would recognize the shift in his demeanor. He needed to buy time to recompose himself. *Excuses,* he thought, *I need an excuse.*

As he opened the front door, Julia King, his mother, immediately rushed towards him with open arms. Waiting by the door for her kids to arrive was her routine. She was perpetually worried for her children when they were not in her sight. She was only relaxed when sunset approached – the regularly-scheduled curfew.

Julia planted a kiss on Stanley's forehead, then she said, "You were almost late, sweetheart. You know your father would have grounded you if you were late again, right?"

Stanley gazed into his mother's vibrant brown eyes, baffled. He expected her to notice his change in character, he expected her to find a microscopic speck of blood on his black jacket. The woman had the eyes of a hawk when it came to cleaning, but she did not notice her son's fracturing psyche. She was clueless.

Stanley grunted to clear his throat, then he said, "I... I lost track of time. That's all. Sorry."

"I tried calling you a few times and you didn't answer. You remember what we told you about answering your phone even when you're with your friends, right? Why didn't you answer? Did you get the calls? Was the service bad? What happened?"

Stanley sighed and shook his head. He still stood on the porch, not one foot in the house, and he was already being interrogated. The passive questioning was irritating. He knew he would be scolded for breaking his phone, too.

Stanley said, "I lost my phone."

The sound of rippling paper emerged from the living room. Stanley peeked inside and spotted the source. Michael King, his father, sat on a forest-green sofa as he read a newspaper. The stern man obviously overheard the conversation. His austere ego would not allow Stanley's mistake to go unpunished.

Michael stood from his seat. With his hands on his hips, he asked, "How the *hell* did you lose your cellphone?"

Stanley shrugged, then he said, "I was in the

woods and–"

Michael interrupted, "What the hell were you doing in the woods?"

Stanley sighed and shook his head. Arguing with his father was pointless. He demanded answers, but he refused to listen to an entire explanation. He only listened until the opportunity to ask another question emerged. He was like a television reporter interviewing a politician. In this case, Stanley was the politician trying to slither away.

Trying to contain the situation, Julia said, "Oh, it's fine. He was due for an upgrade anyway. It's going to be his birthday, too. Cut him some slack."

Michael bit his bottom lip as he stared at his wife. The brunette woman was soft on her children and it irked him. Michael ran his fingers through his grizzled hair as he turned his attention to Stanley. He was willing to scold, but he decided to cut him some slack on his birthday. He sighed, then he flumped into his seat – *whatever.*

Julia patted the dirt from Stanley's jacket and asked, "You want a snack? I can fix something up for you before bed. What do you say?"

Stanley smiled and responded, "No, I want to save some room for *Adventure Planet* tomorrow. I want some funnel cake."

Julia giggled, then she said, "Alright, alright. We'll eat *plenty* of funnel cake tomorrow. Go clean yourself up. Go on."

Stanley nervously smiled as he strolled past his doting mother. He glanced at his preoccupied father and nodded. Except for special days and scolding times, his father was distant. He cared about Stanley's well-being, but he didn't care enough to be involved in the teenager's personal life. There was nothing Stanley could say to change the fact. He walked up the stairs to his left and headed towards his bedroom.

As Stanley reached the top of the steps and stared down the hallway, Daniel King, his older brother, hopped out of the first room to the right. Daniel grabbed his younger brother in a headlock, jerking him every which way. The pair bounced from wall-to-wall as they wrestled.

Daniel said, "Come on, man. What are you doing? Huh? You can't get out of this?"

Through his gritted teeth, Stanley said, "Let me go, asshole."

Daniel shoved Stanley to the floor. Stanley crawled in reverse as he glared at his brother. Daniel closely resembled his younger brother. The siblings had the same vibrant brown eyes and feathery brown hair. The older sibling, however, was taller and stronger. He had a hulking physique, chiseled like a stone sculpture. In a few months, he would finally reach adulthood and graduate from high school. Age and education did not equal maturity, though.

Stanley scowled at Daniel and said, "You're an asshole."

Daniel smirked and said, "Thank you. That means a lot coming from you. Now, why don't you go fuck yourself in your room. We all know what you do in there when you lock the door." As he walked into his room, Daniel chuckled, then he said, "Fucking idiot..."

Stanley staggered to his feet as he huffed and puffed. His brother's bullying antics infuriated him, but he was too weak to respond with action. He shook his head and marched into the neighboring room – his bedroom. He locked the door behind him, then he leaned on the only barrier keeping him away from his family.

Stanley whispered, "Finally..."

***

Stanley removed his jacket and slipped out of his sneakers. He dropped his begrimed jeans, revealing the black basketball shorts he regularly wore underneath. There was a small droplet of dried blood on his white t-shirt. Although puny in scope, the speck was a terrifying reminder of the day. It was not his blood, it was not the result of an accident. It was Richie's blood and it was the outcome of murder.

Stanley walked towards the other end of the room. He glanced around the modest chamber with a furrowed brow, like if he were unfamiliar with his own bedroom. The room belonged to an innocent teenager.

From the horror movie posters clinging to the walls and movie cases stacked beside a flat-screen television, he could see the room belonged to a young man with a love for horrifying fiction. Yet, he couldn't tell for certain if the room belonged to him.

The traumatized teenager sank into the bed at the far end of the room. The smooth navy bed sheets swallowed his body with comfort. The sunset sunshine piercing through the neighboring window caressed his body with a gentle warmth. He rested on a fluffy cloud, floating away from the sick and depraved world.

As he stared at the blank ceiling, Stanley whispered, "Why did I do that? Why did I hurt him? Why did I... Why did I *kill* him? That's not me. That's not who I am, right? I'm not a bad person, am I? Shit, I fucked up..."

Stanley held his trembling hand to his face and sobbed. Saliva spurted through his gritted teeth and mucus dripped from his nostrils. He tried his best to muffle his hysterical cries, wheezing and croaking. The sheer agony was difficult to contain. With each grunt and groan, he saw a flash of Richie's eyes. His friend's fearful gaze rattled him.

Stanley kicked the mattress and muttered, "Richie... Richie... Richie, you fucking idiot, why did you go down there? Why didn't you just listen to me for once in your pathetic life? Huh? Why did you make me do this?"

Stanley wiped the tears from his cheeks and sniffled as he recomposed himself. The emotional pain and fear he felt were whisked away in an instant. He absently stared at the ceiling, watching as a spider skittered across the room. He sighed and shook his head as he realized he was truly apathetic – he did not care.

The tears were nothing but a facade to make himself feel better. He did not feel guilt or pity for his slain friend and the simple fact bothered him. He wanted to feel something, anything, but the emotions would not awaken. His conscience remained dormant, despite his prodding. He felt like a vessel operating on auto-pilot.

Stanley pondered his relationship with Richie, reminiscing about the good times. Despite coming from different families, Richie was a better brother than Daniel. Richie was always willing to offer a helping hand. The young teenager would brawl with a class full of brawny bullies to protect Stanley. Stanley couldn't say the same for himself. Frankly, he didn't care about Richie's untimely death.

Stanley smirked and whispered, "Why didn't I do it earlier? Why didn't I make you squeal like a pig before? Huh? Why didn't I chop you up and feed you to your mom? Why didn't I kill you earlier, asshole? Why didn't—"

Stanley erratically blinked as he snapped out of his vicious tirade. His words and thoughts were vile. He smacked his forehead with his palm, trying to break free from the reprehensible trance. He was baffled, mystified by his shifting character. He thought: *who am I? What am I saying? What's happening to me?*

Teary-eyed, Stanley whispered, "No, no. I didn't mean it, Richie. I never wanted to hurt you... You were my best friend, my *only* friend. Please, forgive me. I'm sorry. I'm so sorry..."

Stanley turned and buried his face in his comfortable pillow. He softly whimpered as he contemplated every word he uttered. His thoughts were muddled. He was lost in a clouded maze, wandering from one dead-end to another. The conflicting emotions made his stomach turn and his brain throb. He wept into his pillow as the sunshine dwindled. Without another word to his parents or brother, he slipped into his nocturnal slumber.

Chapter Four

Welcome to the Family

Stanley shambled through the woodland, searching for the abandoned house. With each cracking twig and groaning branch, he glanced over his shoulder. Only the wind followed him, but he felt a stronger presence – a pair of judgmental eyes watching him from afar. He swallowed the lump clogging his throat, then he glanced up at the sky. The early morning clouds blocked the sun.

Stanley whispered, "It's always cloudy on my birthday..."

The young teenager grunted as he stumbled forward. His eyes widened upon spotting the dilapidated home. To his utter surprise, Ed was already outside. He was dragging two black garbage bags towards the back of the house. Although he could not see through the stuffed bags, he could see strands of human hair protruding from the opening.

Kat simpered as she stood on the porch and watched Stanley. She said, "Ed, it looks like we have a little visitor."

Ed dropped the bags and looked over his shoulder. He said, "It looks like you're right. I sure hope he's alone." He walked towards the rickety porch steps. As he sat on the stairs, he beckoned to Stanley and said, "Come here, boy."

Stanley stood by a tree as he examined the

murderous couple. Although the bags were ominous, the pair did not seem malicious. He couldn't identify the reason behind their actions, but they welcomed him with open arms. The sincere acceptance was strangely reassuring. It was never easy for an introverted teenager to make friends. Stanley's legs wobbled due to the anxiety as he walked towards the porch.

Kat asked, "What are you doing here, sweetheart? You want–"

Ed held his right hand up, calling for silence without uttering a word. He gazed into Stanley's eyes and asked, "You didn't tell anyone about yesterday, did you?" Stanley did not respond – the frog in his throat only allowed him to croak. Ed said, "It would be very stupid of you to do that, boy. Now, I want you to tell me the truth. The truth will let you live. Being honest with yourself, with who you are... *That's liberating.* Believe me, boy, I know it very well. So, tell me: did you tell anyone about yesterday?"

Stanley slowly shook his head and said, "No."

A dead silence followed the blunt response. Ed stared into Stanley's eyes. The windows to his soul were filmy, but he found a decent view. The man was reading the teenager's mind, analyzing his character. The teenager was honest – frightened but *honest.* Ed smirked and nodded – *I believe you, boy.*

Kat leaned on a pillar and said, "That's good, sweetie. I don't see any pigs stampeding through this forest, so I think we can trust you." She placed her index finger on her lips and simpered. She leered at the teen and said, "Well, I don't know, you could be wearing a wire. Maybe we should strip you down and check. You might like it."

As he stared at Stanley, Ed shook his head and said, "Enough of that, Kat. If he's interested in a cougar like yourself, he'll let you know. You see, this is an honest boy we've got here. I can see it in his eyes. It'll take him some time to break free from his chains, but he'll break 'em. Yeah, he'll break free and let loose." He chuckled as he swiped at his nose. He asked, "Now, what are you doing here? How can we help you, St–"

As Ed hesitated, Stanley said, "*Stanley.* My name is Stanley."

"Yeah, yeah, I remember. How can we help you, Stanley? What are you doing back here? We thought you'd run off and forget about this. I was betting you'd kill yourself. I was wrong, though. You're obviously something different."

Kat smirked and said, "Very different and very attractive."

Stanley ran his fingers through his hair as he stepped forward. He was not afraid of the sinister couple, especially since they were not armed. He was afraid of his emotions – or lack thereof. He wanted to explain himself accurately without offending Ed or Kat. His articulation had to be meticulous. *What to say, what to say,* he thought.

Stanley licked his lips, then he said, "I... I wanted to talk to you about something. I–I wanted... I don't know, I wanted to ask you something."

Ed asked, "What is it?"

"Well, I've... I've been feeling *strange* since

yesterday. I've been feeling really sick because... because..."

"Because you killed your chubby friend?"

"Because I don't feel *anything* for my friend. He was my best friend and now he's dead, but I don't feel anything. It makes me scared. I'm... I'm scared of myself, I guess. I don't know how to explain it. It's not normal, is it?"

Ed staggered to his feet, patting the dirt from his jeans and the wrinkles from his shirt. He glanced at Kat with a deadpan expression. The young woman returned the steady face. As the couple turned back towards Stanley, Ed and Kat smiled and chuckled. Their sincere laughter was harmonious, echoing through the woodland.

As he recomposed himself, Ed said, "It's nothing, boy. It's completely normal like morning wood. Like I said, you're breaking free. You're having an... *an awakening.* You're becoming yourself, you understand? The whole 'he was my best friend' bullshit was never real. It was bullshit. What you're feeling now, that's you. That's the *real* you. As long as you don't suppress the new you, you won't feel sick or strange. Trust me."

Stanley shook his head and said, "I don't understand. I didn't want to do that to him. I didn't mean to hurt him. I'm a... I'm a good–"

Kat interrupted, "A good boy? You're still a good boy, sweetie. And, you're still alive. You did what you had to do to survive. That's all that matters. There is no good or bad in this shitty little world of ours. It's just something they tell you to stop you from meeting your full potential. Those *labels* stop you from exploring yourself and becoming who you should be. You understand? They're afraid of people like us because we're not like them. We're free, they're enslaved. We're enlightened, they're stupid."

"*They?*"

Ed explained, "Your parents, law enforcement, the government... The people that create and enforce this 'moral code' bullshit. They want you to live a 'regular' life. They want you to go to school, work a shitty job, get a check, get married, spawn a few pieces of shit, then die. A regularly-scheduled program. Liberal or conservative... that shit doesn't matter. They want to control your life. 'Don't drink too much, don't do drugs, don't have sex, don't kill to relieve your stress.' When you break away from those chains, though, you start to live. There is no good or bad. You're as good as you think you are. You understand?"

Stanley despondently stared down at his muddy sneakers, ingesting the intriguing information. He couldn't tell if the couple were actually enlightened or deranged – or perhaps both. He was willing to accept any explanation as long as he felt better about himself. Murder sat on his shoulders and he yearned to release the heavy burden.

Teary-eyed, Stanley said, "I still killed him, though. I killed someone. I did something very bad and I broke the law. Even if I don't feel it, I know it."

Ed wagged his index finger at the boy and said, "You only 'know' it because that's what they told you. Think about it, boy. If you don't feel *anything* for it, then it wasn't bad. Right? Laws, morals, ethics... It's all bullshit. It's all man-made. How can one man tell us something's bad? Huh? How can another man tell us how to live? *They can't.* You killed someone to survive and you don't feel guilty. That's that. If you liked it, then that's just who you are. That doesn't make you good or bad. It makes you human."

Kat said, "Listen to your gut, sweetie. Don't listen to your parents or the cops, listen to yourself for once. You make your own laws, just like us. Don't force yourself to feel guilty because your 'friend' couldn't survive. And, don't be afraid of yourself, either. If you want blood, you go out there and get blood. You understand?"

Stanley slowly nodded and said, "Yes, ma'am."

"Call me 'Kat,' sweetie. I'm not that old."

Ed smiled and nodded as he approached their visitor. He was content with their discussion, happy to enlighten and inspire. He felt a connection with the young teenager. Although Stanley could not see it, the pair were cut from the same cloth. From their lust for blood to their sheer apathy, Ed and Stanley shared similar traits. Ed simply embraced his deviant desires more than Stanley.

Ed placed his hand on Stanley's shoulder and said, "Boy... Stanley, you are not a bad person. I want you to remember that. You're a survivor, a free spirit. You shouldn't be scared of yourself, you should be embracing it. Fuck good and bad! Fuck the law! Kill the pricks that fuck with you, beat the shit out of anyone looking your way! You feel free to be yourself. You understand me?"

Stanley nodded and said, "I understand. Thank you." He glanced over his shoulder as he thought about his birthday celebration. He said, "I have to go now. It's my birthday, so I have to be with my family."

From the porch, Kat said, "Oh, that sounds like fun. You should have told me it was your birthday, though. I would have taken you inside and made you a man. Too bad. I guess there's always next time..."

Stanley anxiously smiled and murmured, "Yeah, sure."

Ed said, "Go on. Enjoy yourself. Remember what I said: let yourself be free. Whatever you're thinking, *do it.*"

Stanley gazed into Ed's vibrant eyes. He could see the ferocious murderer was genuine. The man was trying to help Stanley feel comfortable with his actions – and it worked. Stanley smiled and nodded in agreement, accepting the advice. His conscience remained dormant, struggling to awaken. He walked towards a tree, then he stopped.

As he watched Stanley with a furrowed brow, Ed asked, "What is it?"

Stanley glanced back at the abandoned house and asked, "Is it okay if I come back sometime?"

Ed huffed and smiled at the innocent question. The request was oddly heartwarming. He glanced back at Kat and softly chuckled. Kat returned the laughter, simpering like a child playing a devious prank. The couple were blessed with joy.

Ed said, "I think I know what you'll say, but I have to ask. What do you think, Kat? Should we welcome him to the family?"

Kat smirked and said, "Of course." She turned towards Stanley and said, "You're welcome to come back any time, sweetie. We've spilled blood together. We're family."

Stanley smiled and nodded. Like the sinister couple, he was overwhelmed by a wave of happiness. He waved at Ed and Kat, then he jogged through the woodland. He glowed with wondrous exuberance, like a child on Christmas. He was a murderer, but his actions were justified. He was a loner, but he was finally accepted.

As he ran, Stanley whispered, "We're family..."

Chapter Five

For His Amusement Only

Stanley shook like a dog out of a bath as he stumbled out of the exit. Water dripped from his soaked hair and drenched t-shirt. He glanced back with wide eyes, watching as the cheerful families and groups of friends meandered down the artificial river. The river rapids ride was teeming with jolly patrons.

Stanley smiled and whispered, "That was awesome."

Daniel slapped the back of Stanley's head and said, "I'm surprised you didn't fall out of the ride, chump. You looked like you were going to cry on that first drop."

"No, I didn't. I got water in my eye."

"Yeah, *right.*"

As Daniel chuckled and walked ahead, Stanley shook his head and indistinctly muttered. Like the roller coaster roaring above him, his emotions were on a thrill ride. One second, he was ecstatic; the next, he was furious. He thought about tripping his brother, but he didn't want to cause a scene. He wanted to avoid embarrassment on his birthday.

As the siblings approached, Julia lifted her shades and said, "I got some pictures of you guys from the bridge. Did you see us?" Daniel and Stanley simultaneously nodded – *yeah.* Julia tapped Daniel's bulging bicep and said, "I'll send them to you in a minute. You can share them with your friends later. I think they'll want to see these."

Daniel said, "Yeah, yeah. Sure..."

Michael wrapped his arm around Julia and joked with Daniel. Stanley ignored the chatter as he examined his father. The stern man wore a striped polo shirt, beach shorts, and black water shoes. His appearance was oddly jumbled, like if he got dressed in the dark – at least partially. He seemed more relaxed than usual, but he was still distant. He didn't notice Stanley's mood swings.

Michael asked, "Hey, kiddo, what do you want to ride next? Hmm? You wanna try out the Shriek-and-Creak?"

Stanley rubbed the nape of his neck and responded, "I don't know..."

Chiming-in, Daniel said, "He's too scared to ride it. Shit, I know he won't do it by himself."

"Oh, settle down, Daniel. Don't tease him on his birthday. You know better than that," Julia scolded. "He doesn't have to ride it if he doesn't want to. Leave him alone."

Michael smiled and said, "Come on, kiddo. I'll ride it with you. What do you say?"

Stanley nervously chuckled as he glanced around the amusement park. He already knew his answer, he was simply caught by surprise. He did not expect the offer from his father. He expected his brother to show a shred of kindness before his own dad. The glance around the park was simply a motion to savor the moment.

Stanley sighed, then he said, "Okay, sure."

"That's my boy. Come on, let's get there before more people show up. You know how this park gets when it's full. We'll be waiting there for hours."

Michael, Julia, and Daniel walked ahead. Stanley followed only a few steps behind. He glanced up at the large ride – the focal point of the park, the Shriek-and-Creak. The metal roller coaster hurtled at breakneck speeds nearing 100 miles per hour. The ride featured steep, long drops and wicked twists and turns. The ferocity of the ride was not nearly as bad as the noise. The patrons' shrill shrieking and the ride's mechanical creaking was nightmarish for a boy with irrational fears. The ride seemed capable of falling apart at a moment's notice, like wet paper.

Michael glanced over his shoulder and said, "Too bad Richie couldn't be here, right, kiddo?"

Julia said, "Oh, that's right. What happened? I thought his mom would let him do anything. That boy is always running around without supervision. Wasn't he going to meet us here?"

Stanley anxiously smiled and rubbed the nape of his neck. He hopped into several rides, devoured funnel cake, and joked with his family all day. Richie didn't cross his mind. He had not thought about his slain friend since the morning he spent with Ed and Kat.

Stanley said, "I don't know what happened. Maybe he got sick or maybe he finally got in trouble. I don't know. I haven't spoken to him in a few days."

Julia furrowed her brow and asked, "Weren't you just with him yesterday?"

"Huh? No, I was going to hang out with him, but I guess he was busy. I don't know. I'll call him when we get home, I guess."

Julia puckered her lips and nodded. She could have pried into Stanley's lies, but she decided to give him a pass. The birthday boy always deserved at least one free pass in the King household. Stanley wondered if he could use it to pardon the murder he committed instead of a fib. It would surely help put his doubt to rest, but it did not seem likely. *Oh, you killed your best friend? Don't worry, sweetie, it's your birthday.*

As he caught a glimpse of the bathroom to his right, Stanley said, "I have to pee. I'll be fast."

Julia said, "Okay, we can wait for you."

Stanley shook his head and said, "No, no. You know how full it gets in the afternoon, right? Just save me a spot in line. I'll sneak up to you guys."

With a raised brow, Michael slowly nodded and said, "Alright, sure. We'll be right up there waiting for you, champ. Don't take too long."

As he walked ahead in reverse, Daniel shouted, "Hey! You better not get us kicked out of line, either!"

Under his breath, Stanley whispered, "Asshole..."

***

Stanley stood at the doorway of the dreary restroom. The gray walls matched the grungy tile flooring. There were four sinks to his right. The mirrors above the sinks were cloudy and cracked. To his left, there were three urinals followed by three stalls. To his utter surprise, the room was empty –

except for the child standing near the urinal.

Stanley stared at the child with a clenched jaw. His thoughts delved into the darkest crevices of his mind, plunging into depravity. Five years younger than Stanley, the black-haired boy was alone and vulnerable. The child was oblivious of Stanley's presence, trying his best to keep his urine in the urinal. He was at an amusement park swamped with people. The boy and his parents obviously felt safe. *What could possibly go wrong in a public space?*

Stanley sniffled as he closed the door behind him. He bit his bottom lip as he realized the door did not have a traditional lock. He could not turn a knob and secure the door, he needed a key from a janitor or a security guard. Yet, the setback was a minor inconvenience to his plans. At the same time, he wasn't absolutely certain about his sinister plot.

As he stared at the door, Stanley whispered, "What am I thinking? I can't do this. I can't do it to him. He's just a kid. He's even younger than me."

As he pulled his zipper up, the boy asked, "Who are you talking to?"

Stanley hopped and gasped, startled by the child's mellifluous voice – sweet like honey streaming down a mountain of sugar. During his self-talk, he didn't realize the boy had finished urinating. The child stared at him with a furrowed brow, baffled by Stanley's erratic behavior. He was not frightened, though, considering Stanley's young age.

Stanley shut his eyes and said, "I'm... I'm not doing anything."

The boy took one step forward and said, "Okay..."

Through his gritted teeth, Stanley said, "Please, just wait a second. Wait, okay? Don't come any closer, kid."

"What?"

"*Don't come any closer.* I need... I need to think about this."

"I was just going to wash my hands. What are you talking about?"

Truth be told, Stanley could not answer the question without sounding insane. His mind was being pummeled by a thousand thoughts a second. Thoughts of blood, violence, and murder stampeded through his fracturing brain, trampling his conscience. *Hurt him, kill him, hurt him,* Stanley thought.

The boy said, "You're scaring me."

Eyes brimming with tears, Stanley scowled and said, "You should be scared of me..."

The boy yelped as Stanley hurtled forward. Stanley struck the kid in the head with a swift jab. He pummeled the child with a barrage of punches – one, two, three, four... *ten.* Stanley was not the most powerful teen, lanky and thin, but each hit was fueled by his hidden savagery. His strength was amplified by his uncontrollable rage.

Dazed by the beating, the child leaned on the urinal and whimpered. Blood dripped from his nose, streaming down his lips and chin. Like a leaky faucet, the blood plopped on the floor – drop-by-drop. A small bruise materialized on his cheek and his nose was swollen. He would certainly survive the beating, but he was in trouble.

Breathing heavily, Stanley asked, "What... What am I doing?" He shook his head and tugged on his hair, throwing a tantrum of confusion. Shifting moods, Stanley glowered and sternly said, "No, I'm not doing anything wrong. This is your fault. You're weak and I'm... I'm just being myself. There's nothing wrong with that. If... If I want blood, I can take it."

Stanley grabbed a fistful of the boy's hair, then he dragged the child into the last stall in the restroom. He pushed the child to the floor. The boy landed beside the toilet. The blood oozing from his nostrils dripped on the grimy tile floor. The stream of blood was not enough to satisfy Stanley's thirst, though.

As he wheezed, Stanley kicked the child's tender face – punting his head like a football. Using all of his body weight, he stomped on the boy's head. The child squirmed and convulsed, then he fell unconscious after the sixth kick. Unconscious was not enough, though. Five brutal kicks followed, each more devastating than the last.

Palms firmly planted on the stall walls, Stanley leaned back and examined the damage. He struggled to catch his breath, gasping for air like a drowning child. As someone usually on the other end of the bullying, the strenuous exercise caught him by surprise. The sudden surge in emotions startled him, too. His conscience was trying to fight back.

Stanley sobbed as he stared at the young boy. The innocent child was brutalized – beaten until he was black and blue. Blood dripped from his nose and gushed from a laceration on his cheek. The child seemed to be breathing, but Stanley could not tell for certain. The boy was limp and unconscious. He snored with each breath, snorting and gurgling.

Teary-eyed, Stanley said, "I'm... I'm sorry. I didn't mean to hurt you. It was an accident, I swear. I don't know what happened. I just lost control of myself. Please, don't tell anyone. Don't tell them it was me..."

Stanley wheezed as he wept. He stumbled into the neighboring stall, immediately staggering to his knees. After a croaking gag, he vomited in the toilet. The chunks of food swirled down the pipe with the push of a lever. As much as the violence made him sick, he was sad to see his funnel cake depart. He rarely indulged in the amusement park delicacy.

Legs like noodles, Stanley returned to the last stall. He gazed at the child and pondered the worrisome situation. Thanks to Ed and Kat, Richie's body would never be discovered. The boy, however, was barely clinging to life in a public bathroom stall. He couldn't flush him down the toilet. *Finish the job,* he thought, *or run.* Juggling the limited options was more difficult than he imagined.

Leaving the child alive would surely cause problems in the future. The boy had a short conversation with his attacker, so he would likely remember his face. On the other hand, killing him would cause a larger media uproar. The boy would not be able to talk, but the police would have a motive to vigorously pursue the case. It was a lose-lose situation.

Stanley held his foot over the boy's throat and said, "I... I have to... I have to put you out of your misery. I have to kill you. That's what I have to do. That's what Ed and Kat would do."

The violent teenager bit his bottom lip as he placed more pressure on the boy's neck. The child barely responded with a shudder as he struggled to breathe. Before he could stomp the child to death, Stanley staggered in reverse. He shook his head as he closed the stall behind him.

Stanley whispered, "I can't do it. I'm sorry. Please, forgive me."

***

The confused teenager shambled towards the sink. The sink generated a garble of noise loud enough to distort his whimpers. He washed his hands and face, trying to rub the blood and filth away with lukewarm water. His time was exhausted. He knew his parents would start searching for him at any second.

Stanley's eyes widened as the restroom door swung open. A man walked into the restroom, smiling and waving at the young teenager – amiable. Nervous, Stanley returned the smile and wave. As the man strolled towards a urinal, unaware of the brutalized child in the stall, Stanley scampered out of the restroom.

Dashing pass the merry families and raucous groups of friends, Stanley sprinted uphill towards the Shriek-and-Creak attraction. He raced through the lanes in his brain, trying to sort through his thoughts. He searched for an excuse – *any excuse.* Adrenaline pumped through his veins. Stanley slowed to a stroll as his family walked down the hill.

With his arms away from his body, Daniel asked, "What the hell happened?"

Julia snapped her fingers at the older sibling and said, "Watch your mouth, Daniel." She turned towards the birthday boy and explained, "We were getting worried, sweetie. I had to pull these two out of line to come looking for you. What happened? What took you so long?"

Stanley sniffled as he quickly examined his family. Daniel was annoyed, Julia was worried, and Michael was indifferent. None of them, however, were suspicious. A white lie could not hurt them like his fists hurt the child in the restroom – a white lie opened his escape route.

Stanley held his hands to his stomach and said, "I'm not feeling good."

Julia pouted and said, "Oh, I'm sorry, sweetheart. What's wrong?"

"My stomach hurts a little. That's all."

Julia nodded and said, "Okay, okay." She glanced at Michael and said, "We should go home. I think it's for the better."

Michael shrugged and said, "Sure, if that's what the kid wants."

"Come on, we barely did anything and the park won't close for a few more hours," Daniel said. He glared at his younger brother and shook his head in disappointment. He patted his mother's shoulder and said, "At least let me stay. You guys go home now and I'll be home before dark. I promise."

Julia wrapped her arm around Stanley and said, "Fine. You better be home before dark. I don't want to stay up all night waiting for you."

Julia, Michael, and Stanley walked towards the exit. Julia coddled her son, rubbing his shoulders and fixing his hair. Stanley ignored her honeyed words. He only thought about the savage beating he inflicted on the child. *Will he survive?*–he thought.

Chapter Six

Contemplation

Stanley sat on his bed and reflected, staring out his window. The falling sun penetrated the overcast sky, dousing the area with a few more minutes of sunshine. Kids scurried across the street, playing in the cul-de-sac. A car horn occasionally broke the jovial ambiance as the working parents returned home. Normality reigned supreme in the neighborhood.

Stanley softly tapped the window and whispered, "What's happening to me? Why did I hurt him? *Why?*"

The young teenager felt like he was trapped in his bedroom – the captive of an insane person. The world continued to move at a normal pace, following the regularly-scheduled program. A young teen was murdered, a child was beaten and taken to the brink of death, but the world did not stop moving. *Would the world stop if they knew the truth?*

Teary-eyed, Stanley whispered, "No one forced me to do it this time. I did it, but I don't know why. Did I... Did I really kill him?" Tears streamed down his blushed cheeks as he sniffled. Stanley nervously smiled and asked, "What's happening to me? Who am I talking to?"

The birthday boy nervously chuckled as he held his knuckle to his mouth. He quietly yelped, then he gazed at his hand. Black and blue, his knuckles were bruising from the beating he dished out. The bruises stung with the slightest touch. Yet, he felt numb to the violence. He was not immune to pain, but he was still struggling to cope with his apathy.

Stanley sank into his bed and stared at the ceiling. He said, "It's not so bad. Maybe they were right. Maybe I'm just different. I'm not a bad person. They just don't understand me. I... I did it because I wanted to do it. I don't have to explain myself to anyone... not even myself."

Stanley flipped on his bed, then he turned on the television. He flipped to channel seven – the local news. The station was broadcasting a report about the presidential election. The report concerned a candidate discussing his penis size. Instead of discussing unemployment, national security, or global warming, reporters and candidates discussed the scientific correlation between the size of a man's hands and his penis. The report seemed like something out of a reality television show.

As far as he could tell, there was no breaking news about Richie or the child at the amusement park. Richie was killed over a day ago and the child was beaten in a public location, but the mainstream media was not concerned with abused children – they were concerned with penises. *If they don't care, why should I?*–Stanley thought. He turned off the television, then he flung the control towards a mountain of laundry at the other side of the room.

Stanley said, "I hope I killed him. Maybe it'll teach his parents to take care of their kid better next time.

Maybe it'll... Maybe it'll *help* them. I killed him. There's nothing wrong with that. I'd kill him again if I had the chance."

Stanley chuckled as he thought about Richie and the child. He imagined his melodramatic mother barging into the room to break the news. He contorted his face, practicing the expression he would use in such an event – saddened, surprised, *amused.* She probably would not notice a difference. With a smirk plastered on his face, Stanley's head swayed as he dozed out of consciousness. *What is it like to sleep?*

In his deepest slumber, he saw nothing. He could not see himself or any other person. He was dreaming about a dark abyss, a void swallowed by an impenetrable darkness. He could hear water in the distance – splashing, plopping, streaming.

Stanley gasped as he awoke. He blinked erratically as he ran his fingers through his hair. With a glance to his right, he could see the sun had vanished – nighttime arrived. To his utter dismay, he could feel his wet underwear and shorts. He glanced down at his crotch and grimaced in disgust. He wet the bed, drenching his clothing and sheets in urine.

Stanley muttered, "Shit..."

The teenager hopped off the bed, pulling the sheets with him. In one swift movement, he pulled down his shorts and underwear. He hid the soiled garments at the bottom of the laundry pile – a mess to deal with at a later time. Like if nothing had happened, he changed into a new set of underwear and shorts. If he did not think about it, perhaps it did not happen – *denial.*

Stanley sat at the edge of the bed and stared at the dusty floor. He whispered, "It was an accident. I drank too much water. That's all. It was not my fault. I'm... I'm a man."

Stanley glanced at the bedroom door as a loud banging sound echoed through the home. The sound of knocking on drywall was persistent.

From downstairs, Michael shouted, "Stanley, get down here! We have to talk to you, boy!"

Wide-eyed, Stanley whispered, "Oh, no..."

***

Stanley sat at the kitchen table, twiddling his thumbs as he glanced around. He was visibly nervous, fidgety like a drug addict suffering from withdrawals. He felt like he was trapped in an interrogation room. Michael leaned on the archway with his arms crossed, Julia sat across the table with her fingers interlocked – the 'good cop, bad cop' routine.

Julia bit her bottom lip, then she said, "Stanley, we got a call from Richie's mother. She told us..." She paused and shut her eyes, trying her best to keep her composure. She said, "I'm sorry. It's just hard to say this to a young man. Your friend, Richie, he's missing. His mother hasn't seen him since yesterday morning."

Michael coughed to clear his throat, then he said, "His mother told us he was with you yesterday. At least, that's what she remembers. You told us you didn't see him. So, what's going on? What's the truth?"

Stanley despondently stared at the hardwood table. He thought about the benefits associated with telling the truth – freedom from his conscience. On the other hand, confessing to murder would likely lead to a criminal case and a stern conviction, which would take away his physical freedom. *I can work around it,* he thought.

Stanley sighed, then he said, "I saw Richie for a while yesterday, but he was acting strange. He wanted to talk to some kids from school. They're bullies. He was acting like them, so I ditched him. That's all."

Michael asked, "Where?"

"It was... It was at the mall. I think he was friends with those kids, so I ditched him. I thought everything was okay. No big deal, right?"

"I thought you said you were in the woods? Remember, you lost your phone or you broke it in the woods? I'm sure you said something like that yesterday. You said you were in the forest, Stanley, don't lie to me."

Stanley nodded and said, "Yeah, yeah... I went to the woods by myself after I left the mall. I just wanted to be by myself. I didn't see Richie for the rest of the day."

Julia tilted her head and gazed into her son's eyes. She asked, "Sweetheart, are you telling the truth?"

Stanley nervously chuckled and nodded – *of course.* He said, "Yes. I don't know what else to say. I mean, I hope he's okay. I wish I could help, but–"

Michael interrupted, "*You can.* Richie's mom already called the police and they're going to start searching tonight and continue throughout the week. Now, you have school tomorrow, but I'm going to take you to Richie's house after. I want you to tell his mom and the cops what you just told us, you understand me?"

Stanley glanced down at the table, strategizing his next move. He couldn't change his father's plan, his words were carved in stone. He could not conjure an excuse, either, or he'd create a maelstrom of suspicion. Before he could utter a word, the front door swung open.

Daniel walked towards the kitchen with his palm planted on his forehead, perplexed. He said, "You... Shit, you won't believe what happened."

Julia shook her head and said, "I don't believe it. You should have been home an hour ago. Where were you? Hmm? Why didn't you answer your phone?"

"I'm sorry. I was at the park, right? Before we could leave, we heard sirens and we saw all of these police officers and paramedics rushing past us. They went into one of the restrooms and they pulled this little boy out. This boy... This boy was beaten *real* bad, dad. I mean, I don't know if he was even breathing."

Astonished, Michael uncrossed his arms and said, "Jesus... What kind of person would do that to a child?"

Eyes swelling with tears, Julia held her trembling hands to her mouth and said, "Please, tell me you're kidding, Daniel. Tell me you're trying to get out of trouble."

Daniel said, "No, I swear. This kid... Man, someone messed him up. I mean, he was a lot younger than Stan. Shit, it was fucked up."

As she walked past her husband and son, Julia said, "Don't curse, Daniel. I hate it when you do that." She walked into the living room and said, "Let's see if it's on TV. I hope that boy is okay. It sounds so horrible."

Michael glanced at Stanley and said, "It sounds like it's going to be a busy week, kiddo. Are you going to be okay?"

With downcast eyes, Stanley responded, "Yeah, sure..."

"You should go get some sleep. Try to clear your mind and relax for a bit. If you need anything, come talk to me."

Michael nodded at his son, then he walked into the living room. The family huddled around the television, flipping through the local news channels. People were drawn to violent and sensationalist media – it was a winning formula.

Stanley remained seated as he watched his family. An epiphany dawned onto him. He realized everyone had a lust for violence and deviant activities, but most people buried their desires – it was 'immoral,' after all. Ed and Kat were correct in their assessment of the world. Stanley did not want to be like his family.

As he stared at his family from the kitchen, Stanley whispered, "I want to be free..."

Chapter Seven

Before School

Gripping a moldering tree trunk, Stanley lunged over a muddy puddle. His black-and-white sneakers were begrimed and mud was splattered on the hem of his jeans. His black t-shirt remained relatively clean. His heavy black backpack made the trek slightly more difficult than usual, but he managed. The bag was filled to the brim with textbooks and notebooks, making his movements stiff and awkward.

As he stared between the cluttered trees, Stanley whispered, "There you are..."

Black smoke clouded the area, undulating towards the gray morning sky. The fumes could barely be seen from afar due to the towering trees. A vile stench wafted through the woodland. The smell was atrocious, like a body decomposing during a scorching summer. The stench of putrefaction was horrendous – it could be used as a perfume to keep people away.

Stanley glanced at the front of the house. Ed and Kat were notably absent. He followed the scent, sniffing and tracking like a police dog. The smoke was the perfect beacon, too, like a black flare. He strolled towards the back of the house. He swallowed loudly as he spotted the source of the smoke and the sickening smell.

Ed and Kat stood around a barbecue pit, holding their shirts to their mouths. The pair gazed at the crepitating pit, hypnotized by the fumes and fire. From afar, Stanley could see the content. Engulfed in blistering flames, a human arm protruded from the pit – burned to a crisp. He was not appalled by the discovery, though. *I wonder if it's Richie's arm in there,* he thought. The young teen coughed to announce himself.

Ed smiled as he spotted their visitor. He said, "Well, look who we've got here. Our boy is back for another visit. I can't say I'm disappointed, boy. I'm surprised, but I'm not disappointed. It's good to see you."

Kat waved at Stanley, wiggling her fingers at the young man. She said, "Hey, sweetie. How was your birthday? I hope no one made you a man before me. That would be a shame." Stanley nervously smiled and shook his head. Kat said, "*Good.* I want you to promise you'll save yourself for me. I have first dibs, okay?"

Stanley said, "Sure..."

Ed spat into the pit, then he said, "So, how was your birthday, boy? I'm sure it was something special. I don't think you'd be here if it wasn't."

Ed and Kat stared at the teenager, attentive like caring parents. Stanley kicked at a clump of dirt, contemplating his response. He was anxious to admit to his dastardly deeds, but the words were clogged in his throat. He swallowed the lump and nodded. He only had so much time before school, so he tackled the problem headfirst.

Stanley said, "I beat up a kid at the amusement park. He was smaller than me and... and something told me to do it, so I did it. I don't know how it happened. I couldn't control myself. I punched him and I kicked him so many times... I think I almost killed him. It was all over the news, too. *Everyone* was talking about it."

Ed huffed, then he said, "I wouldn't worry about the news, boy. They're just feeding the same old bullshit to the public. The people, like your parents, they're going to eat it up for a few days, then they'll forget about it. They'll move onto the next 'big' thing soon. It's always the same shit." He chuckled as he stared at the stark sky. Ed asked, "It felt good, though, didn't it? Beating that boy felt liberating, right?"

Stanley couldn't lie to himself or his newfound mentors. He nodded and said, "I don't know, but it felt better than what I did to Richie."

Kat grinned as she strutted to Stanley's side. The teenager was mesmerized by her swinging hips and bouncing breasts. He wished he could see through her thin blue dress. The garment was tattered and begrimed, but it did not matter to the teen – he was a teenager, after all.

Kat pinched Stanley's cheek and said, "It felt better because you're growing up. You're turning into a *big* boy, hun. I can see you're a *very* big boy. I don't know if I'll be able to keep my paws off of you for much longer, sweetie. You're driving me crazy..."

Stanley rubbed the nape of his neck as he giggled like a boy flirting with his schoolyard crush. He was being teased by an older woman, but it didn't bother him. Ed and Kat joined Stanley's laughter, creating a cacophonous orchestra of clucking. Stanley sat on a wooden bench beside the pit as he stared at the blistering flames. He thought about the burning bodies inside the pit and his lack of remorse and fear. *Is death synonymous with fear?*

Shrugging off his emotions, Stanley said, "I don't really feel like going to school today."

Kat sat beside the boy and asked, "Why not?" Stanley twiddled his fingers, too embarrassed to respond. Kat said, "Now, I usually recommend ditching school. It's a waste of time, believe me, but you don't want to draw attention to yourself now. You don't want to give them a reason to start suspecting you."

Stanley sighed, then he explained, "I don't really care about what I did to Richie 'cause he deserved it. He always dragged me into things I didn't want to do. But, at school, Richie used to help me with some of the... the bullies. Now that he's gone, they're going to gang up on me. I know it's going to happen and I can't do anything to stop it."

Using a branch, Ed shoved the protruding arm into the pit. The blackened arm was swallowed by the flames. He stood on his tiptoes and peered into the pit. The hole was brimming with severed body parts, roasting like beef at a restaurant. From the flames to the dismemberment, the pit seemed to lead straight into hell.

Ed sniffled, then he turned his attention to Stanley. He said, "Well, don't let them bully you, boy.

Small or large, size doesn't matter. You can beat them like you beat that kid at the park. *Don't* let them bully you. It's that simple. You understand?"

Kat caressed Stanley's cheek and said, "He's right."

Pacing in front of the bench, Ed said, "You fight back, boy. You use one of those heavy ass textbooks those dumb fucks at school give you. You stab him with a pencil. *A yellow pencil,* not one of those mechanical pieces of shit. Those will break before you penetrate his skin. You make anything and everything a weapon, you hear me? And, if you can't grab a weapon, you... you kick his knee while you're playing soccer or any other sport. You kick that shit in. 'Oh, it was an accident.' Hell, you don't even have to lie if you don't want to. If they ask you why you did it, you tell them to fuck off. You fight back, boy, it's your right."

Stanley was astonished by Ed's speech. He felt empowered by his wisdom. He killed his best friend, he brought a child to the brink of death. He accomplished more than any schoolyard bully. He was beyond the point of no return, he had broken free from his chains.

Leaning closer to Stanley's ear, Kat whispered, "Fighting back, beating the shit out of punks, that really turns a girl on. It can make any girl wet." She giggled as Stanley blushed. She said, "I'm sorry. You don't even know what that means, do you? You're so cute."

Stanley chuckled as he leaned away. He liked the attention he received from Kat. He was tall, lanky, and introverted. Common high school girls weren't drawn to him like they were to jocks and assholes – a strange magnetic attraction. Yet, sitting on a dilapidated bench and surrounded by burning bodies, he found himself with a woman who cared.

Ed said, "Stop teasing the boy, Kat. I told you, he'll come to you when he's ready. Besides, he's got to head to school and handle his business. Right, son?"

Stanley nodded and said, "Right."

"What are you going to do to those punks if they try anything on you? Huh? What are you going to do to those little bastards?"

"I'm going to... I'm going to fight back. Even if I kill them, I'm going to do what I have to do. It's my *right*."

"That's right! That's my boy!"

Kat rubbed Stanley's shoulder and said, "Don't worry about what they think or what they feel. You go ahead and do whatever you want. And, if you can't handle them, you bring them over here and I'll take care of them for you." As Stanley stood, Kat gave him a gentle spanking. She smirked and said, "Go on. Get out of here."

Stanley gazed into Kat's eyes, then he glanced at Ed. He smiled and said, "Thank you. Thank you for everything."

Chapter Eight

The School

Stanley gazed at the whiteboard, confused. Dozens of numbers and letters were scrawled on the board with black marker. Complex equations teased his mind, taunting his addled brain – *give up, you're stupid.* In Stanley's mind, the numbers and variables were drifting closer together, becoming muddled nonsense. He couldn't make sense of the complicated mathematics.

Mr. Garcia's monotonous voice did not help. The man rambled like a robot with a scripted monologue. His low, dawdling tone only added to the sheer boredom and confusion. The bald spot he tried to hide at the top of his dome was also distracting. The coffee stains on his white button-up shirt and khaki pants were unusual. Stanley could focus on everything but mathematics.

Stanley whispered, "I just don't get it..."

The freshman glanced at the vacant seat to his right – Richie's chair. Without his best friend, the back of the classroom was silent. The pair couldn't make jokes about Garcia's gleaming bald spot – *spit shined every morning, right?* He could not cheat or ask for help, either. He was alone in the back of the classroom, suffering through the lesson without a friend. For a second, he wished to see his chubby pal stuffed into the tiny seat – both for companionship and humor.

Stanley whispered, "At least you don't have to sit through this crap."

Since meeting Ed and Kat, the entire education system became crap in his eyes – *utter bullshit.* He spent hours trying to learn the complex mathematics he was certain he would never use. His mind was being stuffed with useless education, filled with knowledge he would forget before he could escape the short high school walls. *Technology had the answers, education was obsolete.*

Stanley glanced to his left, then he bit his bottom lip. Mark, his personal bully, sat a few seats away. Mark was brawny, strong and nimble. He wore a tight white t-shirt, blue jeans, and black sneakers. He seemed like a regular young man on the surface, but his mind harbored sinister thoughts. He was a brutal bully, beating on the weak and helpless without remorse.

The hulking teenager glanced back at Stanley. He scowled and indistinctly flapped his lips. Stanley could not hear his classmate, but he understood the message. He was an expert at reading lips – at least, he could read Mark's lips with precision. His options were often the same: *I'm going to kick your ass*, *you're a faggot,* or *where's your boyfriend?*

Stanley frowned and shook his head, hoping to defuse the situation. Mark smirked and cracked his knuckles. The popping noise was loud and obnoxious, but the class remained stagnant. Mr. Garcia, lethargic and dull, was unaware of the rampant bullying. *Maybe he's deaf and blind,* Stanley thought, *maybe he doesn't give a fuck.* The latter seemed to be common in school.

Mr. Garcia stood on his tiptoes and stared at Stanley from afar. He asked, "Mr. King, are you paying attention?"

Stanley blinked erratically as he snapped out of his contemplation. He nodded and said, "Yeah, sure."

"Okay, well, what's 'N' in this equation? Hmm?"

Stanley narrowed his eyes as he gazed at the board. Again, the numbers and letters drifted closer together. He could not find an 'n' or a suitable solution. He glanced down at his sheet of paper, dismayed. He had not scribbled a single note since class started. His best bet was to pick a number from the board – any number would do.

Stanley glanced at his teacher and responded, "It's... I don't know. It's 60 or... 76, I guess."

Mr. Garcia huffed and shook his head. He tapped the board with the marker and said, "That's funny since there is no 'N' variable in this equation. So, I wonder what math problems you're working on back there."

With his hand over his mouth, Mark said, "He's probably thinking about his boyfriend."

Most of the class erupted in an orchestra of laughter. Stanley bit his bottom lip as he glanced at each and every teasing peer. The teenagers guffawed like if they had heard a hilarious joke. Homophobia seemed to be popular in the classroom.

Mr. Garcia said, "Settle down, everyone, settle down." As he stared at Stanley, he tapped the board and sternly said, "*Pay attention.*"

With Garcia's dismissal, Stanley realized the education system was, in fact, *crap*. He couldn't help but chuckle. He was surprised by his teacher's indifference. The man scolded a student struggling to learn more than he punished a savage bully. With his nonchalant attitude, Garcia allowed the bullying to spread like an infectious disease. *A bad grade is wrong, bullying is okay.*

Stanley gritted his teeth as he glanced at Mark. His bully childishly simpered as he chattered with his friends. The vicious teen was blatantly proud of himself, stroking his ego in front of an audience. He didn't hide his actions, he showcased his deeds to the world. Mark glanced back at Stanley and winked – a taunt.

Stanley tightly gripped his sharpened yellow pencil. He licked his lips as he stared at the honed tip. The simple piece of wood called for blood and Stanley was happy to respond. He was ready to fight back, regardless of social norms.

Stanley muttered, "I'm not going to let you bully me anymore. I'm stronger than you because I'm free. If I want it, I take it. There's nothing wrong with me... You're going to pay, you fucking asshole. I swear, you're going to pay..."

***

Stanley tossed an empty carton of chocolate milk and a burrito wrapper into the garbage, then he shoved the foam lunch tray into the trash can. His lunch was unhealthy, high in fat and sugar. Much like his math teacher, the school system was indifferent to the physical well-being of the students. The blame could be placed on the faculty or lack of funds, but it did not matter. The menu always remained the same.

Stanley couldn't bother to think about his lunch. He walked out of the loud cafeteria, strolling through the open campus. His peers chattered and bantered at the outdoor tables. Each table represented a different clique, forming clusters of arrogance. Some teens inconspicuously flirted, trying to avoid the security guards and prowling faculty members.

As he walked past the quad, Stanley whispered, "Lucky bastards..."

The young teenager walked towards the back of the school. He found shelter behind a handball court – a towering blue wall erected from the ground. The shade and loneliness offered some comfort. He was tired of the buoyant mood at the school, he wanted to escape his disappointment.

As he flicked pebbles away from the wall, Stanley murmured, "Everyone gets to be happy here except for me. Everyone has friends and... and girlfriends, but I don't. It's not fair." With downcast eyes, he stared up at the overcast sky. He said, "Ed is my friend, Kat likes me. I don't have to be here. It's my life, it's *my* choice."

From around the corner, a male asked, "Who are you talking to, bitch?"

Stanley didn't have to glance towards the voice, he could recognize it in his sleep – *Mark*. Stanley whispered, "Shit..."

As expected, Mark walked around the corner with a smug smile plastered on his face. His gangling lackey stood behind him, constantly chuckling and muttering. The pair stared at Stanley with deviant eyes. Mark had dastardly plans for his feeble peer.

Mark asked, "Where's your fat-ass friend, bitch? I thought he might be in line stuffing his face, but he wasn't there. He wasn't in math, either. So, he must be absent, right? What happened to that asshole?"

I killed him, Stanley wished he could blurt out the confession. He did not feel guilty about it, he was not trying to relieve his conscience. He wanted to claim Richie's death as an achievement. He wanted to strike fear into his enemies. *I killed him and I'm proud,* he thought. Yet, he remained quiet.

Mark said, "You guys spend a lot of time together. I heard you guys have been going into the woods for the past couple of weekends. Spending time alone and shit... What do you guys do out there? Huh? You mess around with him? You like the chubby ones?" Stanley scowled at Mark, insulted by the insinuation. Mark chuckled, then he said, "Look at that, this little faggot thinks he's tough. Bitch, what are you going to do without Richie? Huh? What are you going to do? You going to cry to security like you did last time? Huh?"

Infuriated, Stanley staggered to his feet. He breathed deeply as he clenched his fists. His fingernails pierced his skin, cutting into his palms. He trembled from the rage swelling within. Yet, Mark and his flunky simply laughed at Stanley. They were not threatened by the skinny teenager. They knew him well.

Stanley gritted his teeth, then he rushed forward. He jabbed at Mark's chest, landing a swift punch. To his utter dismay, the jab was useless against Mark's sturdy chest. He didn't have the strength or the form to injure him. The attack was like someone hitting a tree with a twig – worthless, foolish, *humiliating.*

Mark hit Stanley with a quick hook. Caught by surprise, Stanley tumbled to the floor. In an instinctive movement, he immediately wrapped his arms around his head and warped himself into the fetal position. He knew he could not fight back without an advantage. He could kill with Ed's help and he could beat children, but he could not confront a hulking bully.

Mark and his friend did not waste time. The pair pummeled Stanley. The feeble teenager was clobbered with punches to the head and kicks to the gut. He grunted and groaned from the beating, counting each slow and dreadful second – a minute felt like an hour. Mark stomped on Stanley's stomach, then he spat on his face.

As Stanley wiped the gooey saliva from his nose, Mark shouted, "Don't ever try to fuck with me again, you little bitch! I'll fucking kill you! Punk..."

Burying his face in his knees, Stanley couldn't help but chuckle at the threat. Mark had the potential to kill, sure, but he didn't have the heart. Although his bullying was ruthless and obnoxious, he made a foolish mistake – he let Stanley live. Stanley endured years of beatings and name-callings, but he never reached the doorstep of death. *He can't kill me,* he thought.

Stanley watched as his bullies straggled away, shouting vulgar insults with each step. As they turned the corner, Stanley retrieved his wooden pencil. He smirked and groaned as he staggered to his feet. Adrenaline pumped through his veins, vengeance echoed through his mind. He ran up behind Mark, then he thrust the pencil into the bully's lower back. With the weight of his entire body, the sharp pencil penetrated the skin.

As he retracted the pencil, the puncture oozed blood like lava flowing from a volcano. Mark screamed as he lurched forward. Startled, his friend staggered in reverse and watched the commotion with wide eyes. He was willing to beat on the helpless as long as Mark led the way. Without his leader, he was lost and baffled. Stanley glared at the unscathed bully, demanding cooperation without uttering a word – *don't get involved.*

Stanley rushed towards Mark, then he stabbed him again. The pencil punctured Mark's stomach. He twisted the writing utensil inside of his flesh, like if he were sharpening his pencil – amplifying the pain with each turn of his wrist. The bully's white t-shirt was painted red by the gushing blood. Before Stanley could stab him again, the pencil snapped in his hand. Mark sighed in relief, then he tumbled to the floor.

Teary-eyed, Stanley shouted, "I warned you! I told you to leave me alone! Fuck you! *Fuck you!*"

Stanley couldn't throw a strong punch since he did not have the training, but he could certainly land a decent kick. Like if he were playing soccer, Stanley kicked at Mark's face. Mark was dazed by the brutal stomping. A laceration formed on his cheek and his nose was broken from the beating. His face was swelling, like if he were having an allergic reaction.

Breathing heavily, Stanley smirked as a basketball rolled towards him. He grabbed the basketball, then he held it over his head. With all of his might, he flung the basketball down at Mark's face. The *thud* echoed through the court as the pouring blood splattered on the concrete. Before he could strike again, Stanley was pulled back. He glanced over his shoulder and scowled as he spotted the intruding security officer.

Over his rustling navy windbreaker, the officer shouted, "Stop it! Stop!"

Stanley tried to yank away from the officer's grip, but to no avail. Faculty members ran into the basketball court, rushing to aid Mark and restrain Stanley. During his savage attack, he did not notice the crowd of classmates surrounding him. To his utter surprise, his peers appeared appalled. He expected them to cheer for his victorious retaliation – hold him up on their shoulders and parade him through campus. Apparently, fighting back was frowned upon by the group.

Stanley glowered at his classmates and shouted, "Fuck all of you! I hate you!"

Chapter Nine

Consequences

The afternoon sunshine pierced through the fluffy white clouds, beaming down onto the small town. After spending several hours at the high school offices, talking to faculty and police, the King family finally arrived home. The front door rattled as it clashed with the neighboring wall.

With bloodshot eyes, Stanley marched into the home and shouted, "I don't care!"

The young teenager rushed towards the stairs to his left. Before he could escape, Michael grabbed Stanley's backpack and pulled him back into the living room. Stanley tried to squirm away from his father's grip, but to no avail. Even if he could escape from the clutches of his backpack, his father wouldn't allow him to leave without a fight.

Michael sternly said, "*Sit down.* We're not done talking."

Stanley clenched his jaw as he glared at his father. He wanted to strike the man down, topple his dictatorial lead and run free. He knew he wouldn't be able to match his father's strength, though. Without a weapon, he barely put a dent on Mark – he didn't stand a chance against his father. Stanley huffed and crossed his arms, then he flumped into the neighboring sofa.

Michael said, "I don't know what got into you at

school, but don't you *dare* bring it with you here at home. You understand me? I want you to talk to me. I want you to explain yourself. Tell me: why did you attack that boy? What possessed you to act like a *damn* animal at school?"

Julia entered the home, whimpering and shuddering. She had not stopped weeping since she received the news. Daniel followed closely behind, shutting the door with his foot. He rubbed his mother's shoulder, trying to soothe her emotional pain. Stanley watched the pair with a grimace of disgust. He was revolted by Daniel's compassionate behavior.

Michael snapped his fingers and said, "I asked you a question, young man. *Answer me.*"

Stanley responded, "I did it because he was bullying me. He beat me up behind the handball court, so I fought back. There's nothing wrong with that."

"There's nothing wrong with that? You could go to juvie, Stanley! You're suspended and you could get expelled! That will stick with you for the rest of your life! You were dead wrong. Why would you do something like this?"

Jugulars bulging on his throat, Stanley shouted, "I just told you! He was bullying me! He always bullies me and you never care! None of you care!" He sniffled and shook his head, trying to compose himself. He said, "There's nothing wrong with defending myself. I... I didn't do anything wrong. You can't make me feel bad for this. You can't..."

Michael stepped in reverse, baffled by his son's

explanation. He glanced towards his wife and oldest son. Julia leaned on the wall as she wept. She felt her son's anguish through his cracking voice. Daniel simply shrugged at his father. He wasn't aware of Stanley's torment.

Michael turned towards Stanley and said, "You... You can't do something like that because a boy is bullying you. I don't know who told you otherwise, but it's wrong. *It is wrong,* Stanley. You should have told someone."

With a cracking voice, Julia said, "You should have told us, sweetheart. Why didn't you tell us?"

Stanley huffed and rolled his eyes. He said, "I told you before, I told the teachers, I told everyone. I come home with bruises and... and cuts, but you always ignore it. I stood up for myself today. You think it's wrong like everyone else, but I know I did the right thing."

Michael said, "You didn't do the right thing. You can fight back, sure, but not like that. If someone hits you with a rock, you don't shoot back with a gun. No, son, you were wrong here. You *stabbed* one of your classmates. You broke his nose. He's in the emergency room right now. How many times has this boy sent you to the ER? Huh? You took this too far."

"No. You're wrong. It's my right to fight back. And, if... if you don't like it, you can fuck off."

Michael tilted his head and glared at Stanley, astonished by his vulgar vocabulary. He clenched his jaw and his fists as his anger grew. Julia gasped upon hearing her child's demand – *fuck off* – as if the words were as shocking as the violence depicted in the media.

As he stared at his younger brother, baffled and amazed, Daniel whispered, "Oh, shit..."

Michael sighed, then he said, "Go to your room, Stanley. I don't want to see you now. I'll be there in a minute to take away your games, your movies, your TV... *everything.* Get out of my sight, boy. *Go.*"

Stanley remained seated and defiant. He said, "You can't control me anymore. I'm free. I'm free to make my own choices. If I want to do something, I can do it. There is no good or bad. It's all fake. It's all bullshit. Everything I do is only–"

Tired of his son's rambling, Michael pointed at the stairs and barked, "Go to your room, goddammit! Go!"

Michael trembled from the fury he harbored within. He would never admit it, but he had to fight the urge to strike his son. He was never a father of corporal punishment, but his boy's disobedience and insolence irked him to the point of no return. Julia and Daniel had never seen him in such a frustrated state. The pair watched from afar, like if they were watching a live soap opera playing out in their living room – the show was fascinating.

Stanley stood from his seat and said, "I hate you. I hate all of you. I don't care if you hate me, too. Even if you say you don't, I know you do. You're going to pay for this. I'm done being bullied, I'm done being a 'little bitch.' You'll see..."

Stanley sniffled as he walked away. He glanced at his father, his mother, then towards his brother. His family was unnerved by his speech – anger, fear, and confusion reigned supreme. *Mission accomplished,* he thought. He strolled up the stairs without another glance, proudly marching towards his bedroom.

Michael sighed, then he muttered, "Damn it..."

Julia asked, "What... What are we going to do, Michael? He could go to jail for this."

"I don't know. Let's give him a minute to cool off. He didn't mean any of it. I know it hurts, but he didn't mean it. He's just confused. We'll get to the bottom of this. Don't worry."

As he rubbed his mother's shoulders, Daniel said, "Come on, mom. You know he loves you. He's just pissed. Let's get you some tea or some coffee. Come on."

Julia sniffled as she followed her son's lead. She stuttered, "Th–Thank you, honey."

***

Stanley locked his bedroom door. He planted his forehead on the door and whimpered. He was enfeebled by a mishmash of emotions. He meant every word he uttered in his ferocious rant. At the same time, he wanted to retract his statement. The sinister truth was revealed and he would eventually have to face the music.

Stanley muttered, "I hate them... I really hate them. I know they hate me, too. Everyone hates me, except... except Ed and Kat. They understand me. They understand everything." He smiled tenderly as a tear streamed down his cheek. He whispered, "She likes me. She understands me and she really likes me. I know it."

Stanley shambled towards his bed, dragging his feet like if he were trudging through mud. He sat at the corner of his bed and stared at a baseball bat leaning on the dresser. He was never good at sports. He couldn't even hit or catch a baseball. The blue and silver aluminum bat was a symbol of disappointment – a gift from his father. He knew his dad disliked him due to his shortcomings.

As he stared at the bat, blood started to stream from the knob. The blood dribbled down the grip, then the red liquid flowed down the barrel. The rivers of blood dripped down to the end cap of the baseball bat, staining the floor beneath it. Stanley stared at the bloodied bat with a furrowed brow. He wondered, *whose blood is it?*

From over his shoulder, a raspy male voice said, "Your family's blood..."

Stanley gasped as he looked over his shoulder. He stared down at his bed, then he glanced at the sealed window. There was no one in sight. With narrowed eyes, he turned towards the baseball bat. To his utter surprise, the bat was wiped clean. A regular, everyday baseball bat leaned on the dresser.

Stanley stuttered, "Wha–What... What happened to the blood?"

The young teenager shook his head, astonished by the instant change. His breathing intensified as he started to ponder the possibilities. The event seemed surreal, like if he had stumbled into a nightmare. He remembered the argument with his parents, but he couldn't remember if he fell asleep. *A voice and blood,* he thought, *is it me or them?*

The raspy male voice said, "It's us..."

Stanley stumbled to the floor. He glanced at every dim corner of the room, searching for the source of the gravelly voice to no avail. The room was empty. The voice was distinct, but the room was desolate. There were no intruders in sight. Stanley stood on all-fours, then he crawled towards his bed. He leaned towards the ground with his eyes shut.

Like a child scared of the boogeyman, he was afraid to check under the bed. In his search for absolute certainty, the teenager mustered the courage to move forward. He pulled the dangling bed sheets up, then he glanced under the bed. Clumps of dust and a skittering spider harbored the area – nothing more, nothing less.

Stanley stared at the blank ceiling and asked, "Is anyone here? Can you hear me?" There was no response. Stanley stared down at the floor and whispered, "What the hell is happening to me? What's going on here?"

He twirled in place, spinning in the center of his bedroom. He delved into his most wicked thoughts. The blood, the baseball bat, and the voice meant something to him. He simply had to decipher the visuals, he had to decode his thoughts.

As the world spun around him, Stanley asked, "Do you want me to kill them? You want me to kill my mom, my dad, and my brother? Is that what you want?" Although there was no audible response, the teenager nodded as if he were listening to someone. He said, "No, no, I can't do that... I killed my best friend, but I can't kill my family. I'm not strong enough. Not yet..."

Stanley nervously chuckled as he stopped spinning. He staggered to his knees and stared at the floor. His chuckle amplified to a delirious guffaw. The unusual laughter was muddled as he started to sob. He wheezed and groaned as he wept. He tugged on his hair and shook his head. He was breaking down, falling apart like a rocky relationship.

Stanley said, "I want to kill them, I really do, but I don't know how. I need help. I need someone to help me." Trembling like a frightened pup, he wiped the mucus streaming down his lips and moaned. He said, "If I want it, I take it, but I can't do that now. No, I need help. How do I kill them? Huh? With the bat? I'm weak, though. I'm not strong enough to... to crush their *stupid* skulls with it. I have to use a–"

The shrill creak of a floorboard echoed into the room. The floorboards groaned with the slow and heavy steps – someone was approaching. Eyes wide with fear, Stanley stared at the door. Without taking his eyes off the door, he stumbled towards his bed. The ruckus stopped directly outside of his bedroom.

He pushed the blinds aside, then he jumped out of the window. He landed on the shingle roof of the garage. He slowly slid down to the edge of the roof. Like if his fears were whisked away, he inhaled deeply, then he jumped down without a second thought. The two-and-a-half meter fall was surprisingly simple.

Stanley staggered to his feet, wiping the dirt from his jeans, then he sprinted down the sidewalk. He sobbed as he sprinted towards the woodland. The noise around him was muffled, the world was darkened. He didn't see his neighbors' houses, he didn't hear any shouting. He could only see the small house in the forest.

Chapter Ten

A Bond

Stanley stumbled towards the house in the woods, slipping between two trees. His wheezing and coughing echoed through the dreary woodland. From his home to the abandoned house, five miles apart, he didn't stop for a single break. He was exhausted, but he found some relief in the dilapidated house. He stumbled forward, weaving and bobbing his head for a better view of the porch.

Between breaths, Stanley said, "Ed... Ed... Are you guys home? Kat... Kat, I'm here now." There was no response. He inhaled deeply, trying his damnedest to recompose himself, then he said, "Please, I need your help. I need... I need someone to talk to. I can't keep running."

Once again, there was no response. Trees groaned, bushes rustled, twigs snapped, and crows cawed through the woodland. The natural noise was unusually disquieting. Stanley walked up the rickety porch steps, then he stopped in front of the door. He held his clenched fist over the door, waiting for the opportunity to strike.

Stanley whispered, "What if they're not here? What if they were–"

Before he could finish, the door swung open. Kat stood at the doorway, intrigued by Stanley's unexpected visit. She tilted her head and licked her lips as she examined the teenager's perturbed demeanor. Through his appearance, she could see the young teenager was on the edge.

Kat smirked and said, "Look who we've got here." She glanced over her shoulder and shouted, "Ed, bring a few extra beers! Our boy is back for another visit. He looks like he's got some stories to tell. This should be good."

From the kitchen, Ed yelled, "Alright! Sounds good to me!"

Kat held Stanley's hand and said, "Come on and have a seat with us. We were just about to watch the sunset and chug a few beers."

Kat led Stanley to a green sofa on the porch. Stanley couldn't help but smile as he watched her swinging hips and breasts. The woman wore denim short-shorts and a tight white tank top. She had some rosy patches on her skin, but the possible rashes did not bother him. In all her free-spirited glory, the woman was hypnotizing to the boy.

Sitting on the far left, Kat patted the center seat and said, "Come on. Sit down with me, hun."

Stanley took his seat and said, "Thank you. I have to tell you about–"

Interrupting, Ed strolled onto the porch with two six-packs of cheap beer. He took a swig of his beer and smiled. His day seemed to be rather pleasant. He was imperturbable. He flumped into the seat beside Stanley, then he passed a beer to the teenager and Kat.

Ed said, "They're a little warm, but some beer is better than none. Take that as a life lesson. Drink it before it gets warmer, though." He chugged his beer, gulping loudly. He sighed, then he said, "You know how I got these beers? I didn't go over to your big corporate store or any of that bullshit. Some kids, probably a few years older than you, came into our house. They disrespected the land we *rightfully* claimed. They were fucking in here, right? So, me and Kat watched for a moment, we got off, then we slaughtered the bastards. I tore that boy to bits. His little whore didn't fare much better. Believe that. We claim this place as our home and we expect respect. We did nothing wrong. That's the lesson I'm trying to teach you. We did nothing wrong..."

Stanley gazed into Ed's dull eyes. The confession of murder did not rattle him. He was no longer bothered by the couple's actions. He solely wondered if he was one of them. *'I did nothing wrong,'* he thought, *how many times does he say it?* He didn't bother to question him about his conscience. He was still trying to bury his own.

Kat asked, "So, sweetie, you know about our day, what happened during yours? Did you handle those little bastards at school? Or should I expect some company soon?"

Stanley ran his finger across the rim of the can. He said, "I did what you said. I fought back against those assholes. Well, at least one of them... I stabbed him with my pencil two times. Then, I hit him in the face with a basketball. He's in the emergency room now."

Ed chuckled, then he enthusiastically said, "That's my boy. You showed him. You keep showing them, too. Don't let up."

Disregarding the praise, Stanley said, "I... I beat that kid at the amusement park. I still don't know if he's alive or dead. I think I killed him. I'm sure he's dead by now... And, I killed my best friend. So, it's all going to come back to me, isn't it? They're going to find out that I killed them soon, aren't they? They're not just going to let it go."

Ed leaned forward and said, "Now, listen to me, boy. You didn't do anything wrong. The bastard was fighting you and you fought back. You're not wrong because that piece of shit couldn't handle it. Fuck no!"

"It's not that, Ed. I know I was right. I feel good about that. I'm just afraid of getting caught. They're not going to understand me. No one understands me. They're going to send me to juvie, then they'll kill me."

Kat rubbed Stanley's shoulder and said, "Don't speak like that, sweetie. No one is going to kill you. Hell, no one will even *touch* you under my watch. Believe me."

Ed said, "Don't worry about that nonsense. They'll never be able to link you to the murder, boy. Your friend is ash. A pile of ash in the wind, nothing more. They'll need to vacuum this entire forest to find him." He opened Stanley's beer and said, "Drink up, son. It'll calm your nerves."

Stanley clenched his jaw as he glanced down at the beer. He never tasted alcohol before. With Kat and Ed by his side, he wanted to appear experienced – *one of the cool kids.* He sipped the beer like a toddler drinking from a sippy cup. His facade was not very effective, though. Like proud parents, Ed and Kat shared a chuckle as they watched the teenager drink his first beer.

Ed said, "You're part of the family now. If those pigs ever come snooping around, I'll take the fall for you. You just promise you'll keep the bloodline alive. Promise me you'll keep the *spirit* alive. This... This *lifestyle* must continue. There aren't many of us left, unfortunately..."

Stanley could feel the sincerity in the request. He said, "Yeah, I can do that. Thank you."

"Anyway, if you're really afraid of getting caught, you should finish the job the first time. You should close the holes before someone else comes and rips them open."

"What does that mean?"

Ed huffed, then he said, "You know what it means, boy. Don't just attack them, *kill them.* Don't give them the opportunity to point you out. If you're going to do it, then *do it.*" He glanced at the front door and said, "I've got to take a piss and find something to eat. I'll be back, boy."

Ed entered the home, searching for a place to urinate and a body to eat. Seizing the opportunity, Kat leaned closer to Stanley. The toothsome woman grinned as she gently caressed the teenager's cheek. She softly massaged the bruise beneath his left eye. The young teenager shuddered from the pain and excitement.

Kat planted a kiss on his ear, then she sad, "You have to start finishing the job, sweetie. You can beat them up, but that won't end your problems. You have to make sure they never get up again. You have to kill them, put them in the dirt. That's the only way. *Finish the job...*"

With his hands over his crotch, Stanley vacantly stared forward and stuttered, "I–I want to, but... I don't know. I don't think I can do it."

Kat slid her fingertips down Stanley's arms. She drummed her fingers on his hand, then she placed her hand on his thigh. Stanley winced as he felt her warm hand. The woman's gentle touch made him tremble more than any assault from his bullies. He nervously smiled as he tried to keep his composure.

Leaning closer to his ear, Kat whispered, "Maybe you need some motivation..."

From the doorway, Ed asked, "What's going on out here?"

Stanley stammered, "I–I... I wasn't... It–It..."

Kat giggled as she gazed into Stanley's eyes – his anxiety made her excited. She said, "Oh, it's nothing, Ed. I was just giving our boy some advice. Trying to help him see the right way, you know?"

Ed chuckled, then he said, "Sure, sure. I don't think he's ready for you, though. No, I think he should practice on someone else before he moves up to a woman like yourself. You're too wild. You'll make him bust before he's even in. No, he needs time to practice and experiment. Every boy needs time to practice." He beckoned to Stanley and said, "Come here, son. I've got something special for you."

Stanley glanced at Kat, like if he were looking for permission. Kat smirked and nodded – *go on.*

Stanley inhaled deeply, then he walked into the house. Kat followed closely behind. The trio entered the third room in the hall. The troubled teenager stood at the doorway, astonished by his discovery.

Ed said, "Come here, boy. Practice with her."

A young blonde woman laid atop a stained mattress at the other end of the room. Staring into her hollow blue eyes, Stanley could see she was deceased. Judging from the dark bruises on her neck, he believed she was strangled to death. She wore a black t-shirt with a faded bumblebee – the local high school's mascot. Her black leggings were torn at the crotch, revealing her white underwear. Although he suspected she was a fellow student, Stanley couldn't identify her.

Kat walked to Ed's side, then she beckoned to Stanley. She said, "Come on. Have some fun, sweetie. Don't worry, I won't be jealous. I had some fun with her, too."

Stanley nervously smiled as he walked towards the bed. He had a sporadic twitch on his cheek and his fingers trembled. The young woman was stiff like a board, vacantly staring at nothing. Yet, Stanley found himself aroused by the mere sight of her panties. His teeth chattered as he pondered the reasons. He couldn't use teenage hormones to justify his arousal to a murdered teenager. He was depraved and he knew it.

Stanley asked, "What... What do I do?"

Ed smirked and responded, "Well, you should start with a kiss. Maybe grope her breasts while you're at it."

Stanley leaned closer to the woman's face. He admired her chiseled cheekbones and jawline. With a quivering lip, he planted a kiss on her tender lips, then he leaned back. The kiss was not as bad as he expected. With his left hand, he massaged the victim's chest. *They're not bags of sand,* he thought with a gentle smile. As he groped the corpse, he planted another kiss – a seed of sick passion. He couldn't help but chuckle as he leaned back. His first kiss, an often special moment in life, was shared with a corpse.

Kat said, "Move lower, sweetie. Go ahead and slip your fingers under her panties. Make her feel good."

Stanley slid his fingers down the woman's lean torso, inch-by-inch. He licked his lips as he gazed at her panties. He could only imagine what he would feel underneath. His eyes widened as his fingers slipped beneath her underwear. He smiled as he felt her sparse pubic hair. His breathing became erratic and his body trembled.

Ed laughed as he pulled Stanley away from the corpse. He said, "Alright, boy, that's enough. That's what I'm talking about, though. You're not ready for a cold, dead body, so you're not ready for a woman like Kat. Not yet. You'll explode before you even take her clothes off." Kat giggled and shook her head. Ed said, "Don't worry, though. There will be plenty of time to practice. You've got a long life ahead of you."

Stanley nodded and stuttered, "O–Okay..."

Kat said, "Don't be embarrassed about any of this, hun. It's all perfectly natural."

Ed said, "I want you to come out with me for a

moment. Just you and me, you understand? I know you're in trouble with your parents, but I promise you'll be home before sundown. I need to teach you something before you head home. Sound good to you?"

Stanley swallowed the lump in his throat, then he said, "Yeah."

"Good. I think it's about time I show you something special."

Chapter Eleven

A Father-Son Excursion

Stanley followed Ed into the woodland. Ed walked a few meters ahead, lunging over puddles and jostling past the dense bushes. He traversed the gloomy forest with ease. As he trailed the murderer, Stanley glanced over his shoulder. The pair had traveled a mere dozen or so meters away from the house, but the home was already obscured from their view. The house was camouflaged by the environment.

Stanley murmured, "It's the perfect spot..." He hopped as he bumped into Ed. He said, "I'm sorry, I was..."

Ed held his index finger to his lips – *shh.* He whispered, "I want you to keep your voice down for a while. You don't have to whisper, but don't shout." He pointed past a thick shrub and said, "You see this path here? We're going to keep our eyes on it. You understand? I'm going to teach you something very important. Come on."

Ed knelt down behind the shrub. He shoved the leaves aside, creating the perfect vantage point. Stanley followed suit. He knelt down beside Ed, then he peered through the bush. The pair watched a desolate, muddy path – a jogging trail. The trail was eerily vacant, abandoned like the remote house. Only a scampering squirrel occasionally ran across the path. Most sensible people avoided the forest on account of the horror stories and urban legends surrounding the woodland. Stanley didn't even know about the path.

Ed asked, "So, you really like my girl, don't you?" Stanley furrowed his brow and tilted his head, baffled by the question. Ed asked, "You like Kat, right? You think she's a sexy thing, right? You can tell me the truth. Don't be shy."

Stanley stared at his murderous mentor. The man did not take his eyes off the path. Ed was dedicated to his vicious profession. Stanley didn't know how to answer the simple questions. He liked Kat, he found her attractive, but he didn't know what she meant to Ed. He thought, *are they a couple? Are they married?*

Stanley slowly shook his head and said, "I... I don't know. I mean, no, I guess not..."

Ed glanced at Stanley with an unwavering deadpan expression. He asked, "Why? Huh? She ain't good enough for you or something?" Stanley opened his mouth to speak, but he couldn't utter a word – fear caught his tongue and snipped it. Ed smirked and said, "I'm messing with you, boy. It's a joke. That's all. Loosen up a bit. Start embracing your freedom."

Stanley nervously chuckled and nodded – *a joke, sure.* As he composed himself, he asked, "What are we doing here, Ed? What are we supposed be looking at? I don't get it."

"I want to teach you... How do I put this? I want to teach you how to *find* yourself. Spirituality is important in our lives. We're born as free souls, but we become trapped by society. We become frightened of ourselves. You remember those feelings, right? You felt like you did something wrong when you really did nothing at all. You were just living. It's important to embrace our freedoms. It's important to free our spirits."

Stanley asked, "How are you going to teach me that?"

As he stared at the path, Ed said, "I want to teach you how to kill, boy. You're still too scared to act. You're too scared to be yourself. We're going to change that today."

Stanley stared down at himself, mystified. Over the course of three days, he killed a friend, pummeled a child, and stabbed a bully. He was trying his best to embrace his free spirit, but he feared Ed was correct in his analysis. For each one of his actions, he was reluctant to strike. He questioned himself every step of the way. He had the opportunity to kill Mark, he even had the will, but he failed to act.

Stanley asked, "How? How are you going to teach me out here?" Ed glanced at his student with a furrowed brow. Stanley said, "I trust you, but I'm just nervous and–and scared. I just feel like I need to know everything before I actually move on. I'm not *that* scared anymore, especially when I'm around you guys, but I'm just not sure about everything... How are you going to teach me to kill?"

Ed smirked and said, "You'll see, boy, you'll see..."

'You'll see' was not the answer Stanley sought – it was the answer of a slimy presidential candidate slithering away from a tough question. Yet, he refused to pressure his mentor. Wide-eyed, he gazed at the path and patiently waited for his surprise. A minute quickly turned into five. The pair did not share a word as they concentrated on the jogging trail. A cracking twig, a groaning branch, or a scurrying critter couldn't shatter their contemplation.

Stanley narrowed his eyes and leaned forward as he stared at the path, focused. He could hear footsteps from afar, drumming on the moist ground. A raven-haired woman jogged down the trail. Her gray tank top and black running shorts fluttered with the wind. Her ponytail bounced with her majestic movements. She was oblivious of her surroundings. Her music was blaring from her headphones, echoing through the woodland.

Ed grinned as he pulled a serrated knife from his pocket. The knife had a silver handle and a three-inch blade. The knife was puny compared to others, but, in the wrong hands, the blade could cause severe damage. Ed's hands were the worst of all. He spun the tip of the knife on his thumb, cutting into his skin. The small laceration didn't bother him, though. The dripping blood prepared him for the inevitable bloodshed.

As the woman approached, Ed whispered, "She's right on schedule, boy."

***

Stanley could put two and two together. A lonesome, clueless woman running in a desolate forest and a savage serial killer with a knife equaled death and violence. The equation was much easier to solve than his high school mathematics. Still, he couldn't help but hesitate. The answer was on the tip of his tongue, but he could not blurt it out.

Before he could utter a word, Ed chuckled and hurtled out of the bush. He rushed onto the jogging trail, startling the young woman. The woman gasped and hopped, then she gently giggled. For a moment, she believed the confrontation was nothing but a prank – *a joke.* As the woman removed her headphones to converse, she noticed the knife in Ed's hand.

The jogger stepped in reverse and stuttered, "Wha–What are you doing with that?" She glanced around the woods, like if she were searching for a hidden camera crew or a group of obnoxious pranksters. She asked, "What's going on here?"

Ed smirked and said, "Well, little lady, I reckon you fucked up."

Ed grabbed the woman's neck and dragged her off the trail. The jogger flailed her limbs, trying to escape her captor's grip to no avail. Ed placed his sooty hand over her mouth and pulled her towards the bush. The woman's whimpers reverberated through the dreary area, eerie like the cries of a ghost in the mist.

Ed placed the blade on her throat and sternly said, "*Be quiet.* Shut your fucking mouth. You can leave this place, alive and well, as long as you follow my directions. You hear me? I only want to teach my boy a few things about the human body. That's all."

Ed kicked the woman's leg, forcing her to tumble to the ground. He staggered to his knees, then he placed the woman's head on his lap. The jogger wept as she squirmed and glanced around her surroundings. She could see Stanley peeking at her from around a tree. She lifted her head to call for help, then she stopped. She could feel the pressure of the stainless steel blade on her neck.

Ed said, "Don't move too much, darling. Another inch and I'll accidentally cut into your jugular. You won't come back from that. An ambulance won't come save you out here." He glanced up at Stanley and said, "Come out here, boy. Sit over here on her knees to hold her down. Pin her wrists to the ground, too. Make sure she doesn't kick you in your crotch. That will hurt. Believe me."

Stanley swallowed the lump in his throat, like swallowing a golf ball. He reluctantly emerged from behind the tree. He stared at the young woman with teary eyes – she couldn't be much older than a college student straight out of high school. She had an entire life waiting for her.

Yet, the murderous teenager could not show mercy. As the woman slowly shook her head and kicked, Stanley sat on top of her knees. He grabbed both of her wrists and pinned her to the muddy ground, stopping her from swinging.

Ed tossed a matching serrated blade on the ground beside Stanley. He glared at the jogger and said, "I'm going to move my hand. You understand? If you scream, I'm going to kill you. It would be a waste of energy anyway. No one can hear you out here. Don't waste your life." As he wrestled to hold both of the captive's arms with one hand, he said,

"Take the knife. It's yours. It's good for practicing. It's very good for sawing and stabbing. Go on, take it."

Stanley's arm trembled as he grabbed the knife. He stuttered, "Th–Thank you..."

Ed said, "Now, I'm going to show you a few things with this fine lady here. Pay attention, boy." He gently slid the knife across her throat, flirting with death. He said, "There are many ways to kill. Your fists, a pencil, a gun... I prefer a knife. It makes you feel powerful because it's not easy and it's not pretty. I find stabbing straight through the jugular works best. Right through this artery right here. She can bleed to death while gargling her own blood. She won't be able to scream for help and she'll die painfully."

Stanley licked his lips as he stared at the woman's moist throat. He asked, "What if you miss the jugular?"

"Well, as long as you stab her straight through the throat, I think you'll be fine. Get in there deep, though," Ed said. He slid the blade down to her damp chest – her body was drenched in a cold sweat. Ed explained, "You can stab her straight through the heart and kill her instantly. This one has to be a bit more accurate and deep, though. You have to use your entire body, you hear me? If you want to be a bit more playful with the thing, you stab her through the spine. You cripple the bitch, then you have all the fun you want."

The jogger squirmed and wept as she listened to Ed's dastardly advice. Her soft whimpers echoed through the dreary woodland. Ed covered her mouth with his hand, muting her sorrow. The streaming tears could not clean the blood and grime from Ed's fingers. He did not care about his hygiene anyway. He chuckled as he watched her fruitless attempts at escape. She was a source of entertainment – nothing more.

Stanley gazed into the woman's teary eyes. He was staring into unadulterated fear. Yet, he was not concerned with her emotions. He was juggling his options, trying to determine the best course of action. *Throat, heart, spine,* he thought, *or should I try something else?* He figured there was another answer to the equation of death – something to impress his teacher.

As Stanley contemplated, Ed said, "When... When it comes to killing, especially early on, I find it's easier if you're 'acquainted' with your victim. It feels better. It feels *right.*" Ed shoved the woman forward, wrestling with her flailing arms. He said, "Go ahead, boy. You can touch her if you'd like. Touch her anywhere, get to know her. Be one with her spirit."

Through Ed's hand, the woman said in a muffled tone, "Don't... Don't touch me..."

Stanley disregarded her pleas. He heard the words, but the demand translated into muddled nonsense in his mind. He stared at her perky breasts, hypnotized. Over her whimpering, the teenager groped the woman's chest. He squeezed and massaged her breasts; he even dug under her sports bra and tickled her nipples. He giggled like a child on Christmas, excited by his deviant behavior.

In his hypnotic state, Stanley grabbed his trusty knife. He stared at the blade, then he glanced at the jogger. He thrust the blade into her stomach, stabbing directly through her belly button. The woman writhed in pain on the muddy ground, grunting and moaning. Blood squirted from the wound, streaming across her stomach in every direction.

Stanley blinked erratically as he stared at the knife protruding from the jogger's stomach. His breathing intensified as his mind ran wild with uncontrollable thoughts. He couldn't remember stabbing the woman. The knife belonged to him, her blood was smeared on his hands, but he could *not* remember stabbing her.

Over the woman's weeping, Ed said, "Well, I'm glad you went off track, boy. It gives you the chance to learn. This isn't something you'll learn in school, either. It's not in your textbooks or your journals." Ed tapped the protruding knife and said, "Unless you have them chained in a dungeon, you don't want to stab them in the stomach. Not only does it hurt like a motherfucker, but it won't kill them quickly either. Hell, it might not kill them at all. When it comes to stalking on the street, you either kidnap for torture or kill for fun. It's to... It's to get one off before you get home to bust another. You understand?"

Stanley rubbed the nape of his neck and said, "I'm sorry. I don't know what happened. I... I was–"

"Don't apologize. *Never apologize.* You did what you wanted to do. Just remember what I taught you. Now, finish the job."

Stanley inhaled deeply, then he yanked the knife from the woman's stomach. Blood gushed from the puncture, spurting like an erupting volcano. The young teenager crawled forward, trembling as he held the knife. *The jugular,* he thought, *anywhere on the throat.* He gritted his teeth and thrust the blade into the center of the woman's neck.

He missed the jugulars, but the attack was effective. The jogger squirmed as she vacantly stared at the towering trees above. Her vision blurred with each passing second. Blood streamed down her neck, dripping towards her chest. The blood she gargled poured out of her mouth like a waterfall, plopping on her shirt.

Ed removed his hand and said, "*Perfect.* You see what I was talking about? She can't scream. She'll be dead in a minute, maybe less."

Ed grabbed the woman's legs, then he dragged her towards the abandoned house. Stanley followed his mentor as he watched the jogger's suffering. She gazed at Stanley with a vacant stare. She occasionally twitched and jerked. Her involuntary movements only brought her closer to death.

As he dragged the woman, Ed explained, "I've been watching this little lady for a while now. I studied her, you understand? I knew all of her weaknesses, I knew her schedule and her routine. I knew she'd run down that path with her music playing as loud as possible. *You?* Well, I can't tell you what to do, but I can tell you a few things – a few facts. Your family is stopping you from growing and... you know your family's weaknesses. You can finish the job. You can free yourself. You can do it, boy."

Stanley stared at the woman's hollow eyes and whispered, "I can finish the job..."

Chapter Twelve

Before The Storm

Stanley hopped over the brick partition. He landed in the backyard of his home. He glanced at the windows overlooking the kempt backyard. The lights were off on both floors. The area was solely illuminated by the lucent stars and luminous moonlight. He did not see any police lights and he didn't hear any wailing emergency sirens. He was surprised, but he accepted the tranquility as a sign of victory.

Stanley whispered, "They're sleeping... They forgot about me, but at least they're sleeping."

The teenager slowly turned the knob on the back door. He seemed to have hit a lucky streak – the door was left open. He wondered if the door was left unlocked by accident or if it was his mother's doing. Once again, he accepted the unlocked door as a sign of victory – a winning streak. He successfully toppled his powerful father.

Stanley tiptoed into the kitchen, then he carefully shut the door behind him. As he stared at the backyard through the door's window panes, a light illuminated the kitchen. The conniving teenager lowered his head and sighed. *It was too good to be true,* he thought, *it's always too good to be true around here.*

With her fingers wrapped around a mug filled

with hot chocolate, Julia asked, "Where have you been, Stanley? Where did you go? Why would you leave without telling us anything? I just don't... *What has gotten into you, boy?*"

Stanley glanced over his shoulder. His mother sat at the kitchen table, sniffling and shuddering. He could tell she had spent the afternoon crying. His father leaned on the archway with his arms crossed, dour. The man seemed calmer than before, though.

Michael said, "Sit down and answer your mother."

Stanley stared at his father, then he loudly swallowed – the gulp practically echoed through the house. He sat directly across from his mother, staring into her puffy eyes. He was too frightened to explain himself. He wouldn't confess to his sinister deeds. He cycled through his excuses, searching for the perfect fit.

Julia asked, "Why are you acting like this? What's wrong, sweetheart?"

Stanley shrugged and said, "Nothing... I just... I just needed some fresh air. I needed to think about what I did and what I said to you. I was wrong about all of that. I'm sorry about everything. I was just... I was tired of Mark bullying me and I was tired of you ignoring me. I was tired of everything. That's all."

Julia grimaced from the emotional pain. She said, "I'm so sorry, sweetheart. I would never do that on purpose. You know I'm *always* here to listen. You know that, don't you?"

"Yeah, but you never do anything about it. None of you do anything about it. You used to ask me about my bruises and my dirty clothes, then you started to ignore everything. You just stopped asking. You cared, but you really didn't..."

Michael said, "We always cared. I guess we lost track for a moment. We messed up, kiddo. I'm sorry about that. It might be too little, too late, but I'll be heading to the school to talk to them about your bullying problem. I want to get to the bottom of this. I want to understand why you did this and what we can do to prevent it from happening again."

Stanley could hear the remorse in his father's voice. For the first time in years, he could see his father cared about his well-being. From her sincere tears, he could see his mother was also concerned. The ambiance shifted from dreary to amiable. Yet, the teenager felt patronized. *Why does he have to talk to the school? Doesn't he believe me?*–he thought.

Stanley said, "I told you why I did it. I was defending myself. Mark and his friend punched and kicked me, so I fought back. Can't you... Can't you see all of my bruises?" Julia and Michael stared at their son, examining his physical and emotional condition. Stanley shook his head and said, "You never take my side anyway. He could have killed me and you'd still blame me."

Julia said, "Don't talk like that. Please, don't ever say that again. You know it's not true, sweetheart."

"*It is.*"

Michael rubbed his eyes with his thumb and index finger. He sniffled and shook his head, downhearted. He was utterly disappointed in himself. He felt his strict and uncompromising parenting facilitated Stanley's pain. Stanley stared at his father with narrowed eyes, perplexed. He felt a strange, inexplicable sensation flowing through his body. He had not experienced genuine sympathy in days. He questioned his emotions, but he did not act on them.

Michael said, "In a sense, I guess you're right. Don't blame your mother, though. It's my fault and I take full responsibility. It was... *It was me.* I want to spend more time with you from now on, Stanley. You understand? I want to be there for you when you need me. Let's go watch a ball game or go to the park. Let's do something together. Let's get reacquainted. Does that sound good to you?"

Stanley gazed into his father's eyes – he could see his glistening tears. He said, "Yeah, sure. That sounds good."

"Good, good... I'll do better, champ, I promise. We'll get through this together."

Julia planted her fingertips on Stanley's hand and said, "We will *all* get through this, sweetheart. We'll always be there for you. I'm sorry for everything. I'm so sorry."

As his eyes swelled with tears, Stanley said, "I'm sorry, too. I'm sorry for everything I did and everything I said. It was stupid. I didn't mean it."

Stanley stood from his seat, then he lurched towards his father. His father was surprised by Stanley's warm hug. He patted his son's shoulder and smiled. Julia joined from behind, embracing her husband and son.

Julia planted a kiss on the back of Stanley's head, then she said, "Please, don't ever run away like that again. You had me so worried, baby. We called all of your classmates and our neighbors. We even called the police. Please, don't do that again. I don't think my heart can take it."

Stanley stepped out of the hug. He asked, "You called the cops?"

Michael sighed, then he explained, "Yeah. They were here an hour ago. I'll call them and let them know you're back."

Stanley murmured, "Okay, okay..."

"That reminds me, kiddo. We won't be able to go out tomorrow, at least not right away. You still have to talk to the police about your little friend. I know it's a difficult time right now, but they're going to need your help. You need to stay strong, alright? You need to be there for Richie and his mom."

Julia stroked Stanley's hair and said, "Don't worry, sweetheart. He's going to be fine. I promise, we're going to find Richie and you'll be able to spend time with him again. I know it." Stanley clenched his jaw and stared at his mother, trying to contain his rage. Julia said, "You should go up and get some sleep. You've had a busy week. You're going to need some rest. Go on. I love you."

Michael nodded and said, "Good night, kiddo. I'll see you in the morning."

Stanley's breathing intensified as he stared at his parents. He was infuriated by their prying actions. He could barely outmaneuver his parents, his chances were slim against the police. Stanley bit his bottom lip and walked out of the kitchen. He strolled towards his bedroom, lost in his dreadful thoughts.

Chapter Thirteen

Blind Bloodshed

Stanley wheezed as he awoke, gasping for air and drenched in sweat. Shocked, he crawled in reverse on his bed and glanced around his room. The moonlight pouring through the slits in the blinds barely illuminated the dark bedroom. The ominous shadows swayed through the room, like mist dancing with the wind.

Stanley whispered, "What's happening? What... What's going on here?"

He swallowed the lump in his throat as he rapidly blinked. He glanced down at his crotch with wide eyes. Through the darkness, he could see the contrasting color on his navy comforter – a blatant dark spot. Like a magician revealing his trick, the teenager pulled the comforter from his body. He was baffled by his discovery.

Stanley muttered, "I didn't do this... No, it wasn't me."

His navy flannel pajama bottoms and the bed sheets were soaked in urine. His crotch was damp and warm. The tawny piss stained the bed and the garment with a pungent stench. To his utter dismay, the urine was fresh and plentiful. His accident was difficult to deny, but he could not accept it. The humiliation paralyzed him.

Stanley sniffled and said, "No, not again... It wasn't

me. It... It wasn't me, damn it!"

Stanley's head swayed as he glanced around the bedroom. The shadows were whisked away, like a bank of fog dissipating during a summer morning. The walls seemed to be melting. He could see the blue paint dribbling down the walls in large clumps. Steam billowed from the floor, undulating towards the ceiling. The *entire* room seemed to be melting before his very eyes. Although the illusion felt tangible, the experience was surreal.

Stanley tightly shut his eyes and whispered, "It's a nightmare, it's a nightmare, it's a nightmare..." As he opened his eyes, he sternly repeated, "*It's a nightmare.*"

The teenager sighed in relief as the room returned to its normal state. He sat at the edge of his bed and pondered the strange experience. Only one thought ran through his mind: *melting, melting, melting.* He tried to decipher the uncanny vision, but to no avail. He didn't have the knowledge or experience to fully understand himself.

Stanley staggered to his feet, then he shambled towards a mountain of dirty laundry next to his dresser. The pile emitted a revolting stench, but he had already grown accustomed to it. He yanked his jeans from the mound, causing an avalanche of clothing to fall over. His legs wobbled as he searched through his pockets – a result of exhaustion and disbelief.

Upon finding his trusty knife, Stanley whispered, "I can finish the job. I know their weaknesses. I can do it."

The impressionable teenager gazed at the knife, examining the serrated blade with a set of deviant eyes. The jagged edge of the knife was hypnotizing, like the serrated teeth of a shark. Blood oozed from the tip of the knife, streaming down the sturdy blade. The blood was unusually tantalizing, like whiskey to an alcoholic. With the blink of an eye, the blood vanished.

Stanley said, "It's time..."

***

Stanley shambled into the hall with slumped shoulders, dragging his feet like a child dragged to the mall. He glanced at the room to his left – Daniel's room – then he stared down the hall to his right. His parents claimed the last room in the hall as their master chamber. His father's snoring could be heard from anywhere in the house.

The teen erratically blinked and sniffled as he planned his strategy. To murder his parents, he required speed and accuracy. If he failed, his brother would awaken and foil his plot. He knew he could not handle his brother in a brawl – with or without a weapon. *Kill the asshole first,* he thought, *then kill the rest.*

He stood at the doorway of his brother's bedroom. He glanced around the room, reminiscing about the past. He remembered sitting towards the center of the room and playing video games with his brother. The pair would fight for the first-player controller. Of course, Daniel would win nine times out of ten. The memory was tender, bringing a tear to his eye. He wiped the tear and shrugged off the beautiful memories.

Stanley tiptoed into the room, calculating every step. He carefully walked over the tube socks and food wrappers littered across the floor. His brother's natural habitat was polluted by garbage. Their parents did not seem to care about his bedroom, though. Unlike his younger sibling, Daniel had some privacy in the house. Michael and Julia respected him as a young man.

A nudie poster above Daniel's bed caught Stanley's eye. The image depicted a blonde woman with a large bosom and bushy pubic hair. She seductively licked her index finger while partially covering her crotch with her other hand. Stanley couldn't help but chuckle – he preferred the *real* thing to simple pornographic imagery.

Stanley stood beside the bed, staring at his slumbering brother. Without a snore or squirm, Daniel slept peacefully. He was blissfully unaware of his brother's psychotic breakdown, sleeping through the madness.

Stanley whispered, "What are you dreaming about? What's more important than me? Huh? Cars? Money? *Girls?*" Staring at Daniel's bare throat, Stanley placed the tip of the blade on his Adam's apple. Stanley licked his lips, then he whispered, "What are you dreaming about?"

Using all of his body weight, Stanley stabbed the blade into Daniel's throat. Daniel awoke with wide eyes, flopping on the bed like a fish out of water. He flailed his limbs and violently convulsed. Despite his strong urge and his modest attempts, he could not scream. He could only gargle and spit blood. He grabbed Stanley's wrist and gazed into his little brother's eyes, shocked.

Stanley huffed, then he slowly twisted the blade. Blood squirted from the wound as the laceration widened – spurting like a garden sprinkler. The gushing puncture splattered Stanley with droplets of blood. The blood stained his face and his clothing, spattered across his body like red paint. He was unperturbed by the savagery as he continued to twist the blade.

Through his gritted teeth, Stanley said, "*Fuck you.*"

Stanley stumbled back as he yanked the blade out with all of his might, like if he were pulling a legendary sword from a sturdy stone. He gazed at his brother, memorizing each twitch and moan. He wanted to remember the vivid portrait of death – a portrait painted by his own malign hands – *a masterpiece.*

With bloodshot eyes, Daniel returned the gaze. He was shocked and bewildered by the violent attack, trying to catch the slightest breath of air. He stared at his murderous sibling as he held the grisly puncture on his throat. He knew he could not stop the excessive bleeding, but human instinct told him to try. With one final exhale, Daniel passed away.

Stanley smirked as he stared into his brother's eyes. He watched as the life vanished from his body. Although he physically remained the same, he could see the energy – *the soul* – depart from his body. He had seen death in hollow eyes before, but he was finally able to savor the experience. He killed him on his own and he was proud of it.

The violent teenager said, "Maybe we'll see each other again someday, Daniel. If it really exists, both of us can play video games and... and try smoking cigarettes in hell. It's where we'll both end up, but you knew that already, right? We're... We're bastards."

***

Stanley stood towards the center of the hallway, staring at his parents' bedroom door. His father's sputtering snores reverberated through the home. A drop of blood occasionally plopped on the ground, like water dripping from a leaky faucet. The floorboards groaned beneath his feet, echoing like the cries of a beaten man. Despite the ruckus, Michael and Anna continued to sleep.

Stanley whispered, "I didn't want to do it. I really didn't mean it, but I... I have to finish the job. I don't want to go to jail. I want to live free. I'm not bad, I'm just... I don't know what I am. I just know I have to finish the job."

Stanley trudged down the hallway, plodding towards the master bedroom. He slowly turned the knob, then he shoved the door open. He grimaced as the hinges squealed like a pig in mud. He knew about the squeaky door, but he didn't realize it would be so obnoxious during a silent night. To his utter surprise, his parents did not awaken.

The young teenager couldn't help but smile smugly as he stared at his parents. His parents slept on a queen-sized mattress towards the center of the room. There was a nightstand to the left and right, each with a matching lamp. The couple were veiled by a thick crimson comforter – darker than Daniel's blood.

Julia slept on the left side of the mattress. Her hair was tied in a tousled bun, strands protruding every which way. She was knocked out on her stomach, likely tranquilized by sleeping pills. The sleeping pills were not used due to Stanley's bad behavior, though. The pills were part of her nightly routine. In her current condition, the woman could sleep through a ruinous earthquake – or her son's violent death.

Michael slept on the right side of the mattress, laying on his back. He snored like a bear in hibernation. Each croaky snore crepitated like a struggling engine. Unlike his beloved wife, the man was simply exhausted – a hard day's work took a toll on him. He didn't need sleeping pills to aid him in his quest for a peaceful slumber.

Stanley stood beside his father, staring down at him. He felt powerful towering over the man. He could see the saliva dripping down his father's cheek, soaking the comfy pillow. He was as oblivious as Daniel before the young man's brutal death. Like Ed said, Stanley knew their vulnerabilities. Sleep was their unfortunate weakness.

Stanley inhaled deeply, then he thrust the knife into his father's neck. Michael bounced on the bed as the blade penetrated his jugular. Wide-eyed, he stared at his son in utter disbelief. Stanley yelped as his father tightly gripped his forearm. The violent teenager tried to stagger away, but his father refused to release him. Even with a blade jammed into his throat, the man was strong.

Stanley sternly said, "Let me go. Let me go. *Let me go!*"

Michael grunted and groaned as blood oozed from his mouth, foaming with his saliva. He slowly blinked and shook his head, dazed by the loss of blood. In an effort to save himself, he flung his arm at his slumbering wife. She didn't awaken from the strike. He slapped her bottom with all of the energy he could conjure – three consecutive spankings.

Without lifting her head, Julia groaned, then she asked, "What do you want?" She could hear a gurgling sound and she felt the bed trembling. She furrowed her brow and asked, "What are you doing, sweetie?"

Julia sniffled as she nonchalantly reached for the lamp – she wasn't in a hurry. As the dusty bulb illuminated the bed, Julia glanced over at her husband. She blinked and rubbed her eyes, then she gasped – a loud, raspy inhale. She trembled as she watched her husband, shocked. Upon spotting her bloodied son, she screamed at the top of her lungs. Her shrill shriek echoed through the home, reverberating through the neighborhood.

Distraught and fidgety, Stanley pulled the knife from his father's throat. As Julia tumbled off the bed, Stanley leaped onto her. He held the knife over his head, then he stabbed his mother's back. The knife penetrated Julia's spine at the small of her back. Wide-eyed, Julia stopped and wheezed, breathing throatily as she tried to cling to life.

Stanley pulled the knife out, then he flumped onto the bed. He sat at the corner of the mattress, watching his mother's hopeless movements. He could see her insufferable pain as she violently convulsed. The floorboards groaned as she writhed in agony on the ground. *I have to finish the job,* he thought, *I have to put her out of her misery.*

As she crawled in reverse, dragging her limp legs, Julia stuttered, "Pl–Please... Please don't... D–Don't..." She wept hysterically as her arms gave out. She could not crawl any farther. Teary-eyed, she said, "Don't... Don't do this. I love you, sweetie."

Stanley's bottom lip quivered as the words struck him like the jabs from a heavyweight boxer. His emotions were uncontrollable – from blind rage to sincere love. Although he sought to finish the job, he struggled to murder his mother. His mother may have been an enabler, but she genuinely loved her children. She never meant any harm. *Does she deserve it?*–Stanley thought.

From over his shoulder, a raspy voice whispered, "She does..."

Stanley quickly staggered to his feet and glanced back. There was no one behind him. He glanced down at his father, pondering the possibility. Michael barely squirmed on the bed. He tried to move, but he was enfeebled by the stabbing. With the gaping hole in his throat, he couldn't possibly be the source of the voice.

Stanley stared at the wall behind him and asked, "She does deserve it, doesn't she? Th–This is her fault, right?"

As her teeth chattered, Julia stuttered, "Wh–Who are you talking to, sweetie?"

Stanley glared at his mother, piercing into her soul. He huffed and puffed as he marched towards Julia. Julia cried as she tried to wiggle away, but she was immobilized by her spinal injury. Stanley lifted his knee to his stomach, then he stomped on her neck with all of his might. Julia was silenced with her crushed throat.

The young teenager whispered, "I love you, too."

***

Stanley gazed into his mother's hollow eyes. He smirked as he glanced down at her throat. He left an indentation the size of his heel on her neck, like a wide dimple. The teenager deliriously giggled as he stared at his father's mutilated throat. The brutality of the murders was oddly amusing. His parents were dead and he could not stop laughing.

He shook his head as he walked out of the bedroom. He strolled down the hall, then he peeked into Daniel's bedroom. His brother's death brought a smile to his face. He skipped through the house, capering like a child at the park. He rushed into the basement and grabbed two red canisters of gasoline. He remembered his father's explanation – *this is only for emergencies.*

As he spilled the pungent fluid through the house, Stanley whispered, "This *is* an emergency, dad. I have to make sure no one ever finds out about it. I have to finish the job. I'm sorry for using your gas. I'll make sure to pay you back when I get a real job."

Although he had a limited supply, the home was

successfully doused in fuel. He was not a professional arsonist, but he often spent time playing with fire. He knew the flames would spread in time, so he focused the fuel on key areas. He drenched the hallways, the doorways, and any flammable furniture. He made sure to soak his brother's carcass, too. He wanted to burn the most significant evidence – *the bodies.*

As he returned to the master bedroom, Stanley said, "I know we were supposed to... to get better, but I can't. I know now that I'm *not* like all of you. I'm free and you don't like that. So, I'm going to set you free, too. Okay? It's better like this."

Stanley sniffled as he poured gasoline on his father's body. He lugged the canister towards his mother, then he dumped the remaining fluid. He glanced at the floorboards, making sure the flammable trail was well-defined. His preparations were far from perfect, but the plot seemed feasible. In the teenager's mind, fire meant destruction – and destruction would leave nothing in its wake.

Stanley glanced at his mother and whispered, "I really did love you, mom. I'm sorry..."

Stanley sobbed as he ran through the house, lunging over the trail of gasoline he meticulously crafted. He wept from his mixed emotions. He felt sympathetic due to his actions and happy due to his liberation – an unnerving contradiction. He stumbled into the kitchen, then he retrieved a matchbook from a drawer. Since he was a child, he preferred matches to action figures. *Why pretend to shoot a flamethrower when you can play with real fire?*

He whispered, "This is it. This is how I finish it. This is what Ed and Kat were talking about." He glanced at the ceiling with despondent eyes. He shook his head and whispered, "No, no, I can't stop it. I have to finish it. There's no turning back. I'm sorry."

Stanley staggered towards the front door. From the porch, he lit a match, then he tossed the burning stick into the house. He watched as the flames quickly spread through the home. He waited until the crepitating flames danced up the stairs. Stanley wiped the tears from his cheeks. He continuously glanced back at the house as he slowly walked away. He could see the flickering flames through the windows. The fire began to swallow every room in the house.

Although he wanted to wait until the house crumbled, he knew he would have to depart before the fire department and police arrived. A lone survivor and a suspicious fire never looked good. He refused to be taken into custody – as a victim or a suspect. Barefooted and in his pajamas, Stanley ran down the street, sprinting towards the woodland.

Chapter Fourteen

A New Man with a New Family

Stanley shivered as he stared at the abandoned house – *a new home.* He crossed his arms and rubbed his shoulders as he strolled towards the remote building. Although he had visited the house many times before, he couldn't be more confused and frightened. His barbarous actions tainted his mind and crippled his psyche. Uncertainty reigned supreme.

The young teenager shoved the front door. As expected, the door was left open. The couple didn't see the need to lock their doors or hide their dastardly deeds. They proudly took refuge in the abandoned house, displaying their deviant activities for the world to see. The pair were a paradigm for modern serial killers.

Standing at the archway, Stanley gazed at the filthy couch in the living room. Ed and Kat shared the sofa, sleeping peacefully on the grime. Ed did not utter a sound, sleeping as stiff as a board. Kat's snore vibrated like a cat's purr – *appropriate.* Stanley loudly coughed and grunted, purposely trying to wake the pair.

Ed glanced over his shoulder, then he narrowed his eyes. He gently shoved Kat and said, "Wake up, girl. It looks like we've got some company."

Kat lightly slapped Ed's sturdy chest and said,

"Five more minutes..."

"No, no. I think you'll want to see this. Come on, get up."

Ed staggered to his feet as he quickly lifted his jeans to his waist. He grabbed his white wife beater from the floor, then he tossed the garment over his head. As he sloppily dressed himself in his victims' clothing, the killer carefully examined Stanley's peculiar demeanor. Through the midnight darkness, he could see the blood on the teen's face and pajamas.

Ed asked, "How are you doing, boy?"

With glum eyes, Stanley responded, "I... I don't know."

Kat's eyes widened upon hearing the teen's tender voice. She hopped up from the sofa, smirking as she turned towards the archway. Her devious grin was wiped from her face as she spotted the blood. She could see the teenager had been through a harrowing experience. Doused in blood, he wreaked havoc and escaped his chains.

Stanley, on the other hand, anxiously smiled as he watched Kat. Kat slept in her white brassiere and a flimsy thong. In his eyes, she was practically nude. From her bosom to her crotch, he couldn't help but ogle. He had murdered his family only moments ago and the view of Kat's body was the best stress reliever.

Ed snapped his fingers and said, "*Hey*. Listen, you don't have to talk about it. You understand me? That's one of the benefits of being a free man. You *don't* have to talk about it. I'm here to listen to you, boy, but only if you want to talk. It's your choice."

Stanley nodded and said, "I... I don't know why I did it. I don't... I don't even remember what I did, Ed. It's all messed up in my brain."

Ed clenched his jaw and glanced at Kat – the pair communicated through their eyes. Ed said, "I know what you did, boy. We both know what you did. And, if I may be a little sentimental, I must say I'm proud of you. You finished the job. You liberated yourself, son. You broke the chains without anyone's help. *You're free.* Shit, boy, you're my hero."

Kat giggled, then she said, "You're my hero, too, Stanley. You're... *You're amazing.* I've never met anyone like you before. Well, maybe one person..."

Stanley's eye twitched as he smiled. The praise and acceptance caught him by surprise. He wasn't criticized or punished for his wicked actions. The couple welcomed him with open arms, showing more affection than his own blood. Defending himself against bullies brought nothing but trouble to his family. In the abandoned house, he felt appreciated.

Ed said, "Let's get you cleaned up. We've got to get that blood off of you. Go out to the backyard and undress yourself. I'll be out in a minute."

The teenager bit his bottom lip and gave a slight nod. He was nervous about disrobing in front of the couple, but he trusted Ed. As far as he could tell, he was not led astray yet. He needed to wash his family's blood off his body – it was undeniable. He walked out of the back door, stopping near the barbecue pit. Peering into the pit, he could see it was recently cleaned. *The bodies are gone,* he thought, *where's Richie?*

Stanley sniffled as he slowly unbuttoned his flannel shirt. He tossed the shirt on the edge of the pit. He dropped his pants to his ankles, then he gasped. He knew Kat was watching from the door. Her leering made him nervous, but she didn't bother him. The urine stain on his boxers was humiliating, though. Although he was nervous to strip in front of the murderous woman, he did not have many options on the table. He quickly tossed his boxers down the pit, then he turned away.

Stanley whispered, "Shit, shit, shit. Did she... Did she see it?"

As he walked towards the back door, Ed glanced at Kat and asked, "What are you doing, girl?"

Kat simpered, then she said, "Well, he's putting on a show out there. What do you expect me to do? *Miss it?*"

"I expect you to give him some privacy after what he's been through. You know better than that."

"I know, I know, but I think he likes it. I think he wants me to watch. If he's feeling bad, you know I can make him feel good. It's my specialty."

Ed huffed and shook his head as he walked out of the house – *this woman is something else.* He held two buckets brimming with water in his hands. Upon spotting the teen's pale buttocks, he couldn't help but chuckle. Stanley shivered as he glanced at his mentor.

Ed said, "I'm going to dump some water on you. Don't worry, it's clean. We got it from the creek.

Might be a little cold, though. Rub yourself down 'cause I ain't doing that for you and I still don't think you're ready for Kat. She's over there ready to claw into you, boy. I mean it, too. That woman will *claw* into you."

From the doorway, Kat said, "I can hear you."

"*Good.* You should start a fire. The boy's going to have to warm up in a minute. Find him a blanket or a towel, too. We'll be finished soon."

Kat sighed, then she said, "Alright, alright..."

Stanley shuddered as the cold water was poured onto his head. The water streamed down his face and neck, quickly coursing down his entire body. He vigorously rubbed his body, trying to clean himself while also conjuring some warmth. His family's blood was washed away with the second bucket, blending with the mud. Kat strutted out of the home, still in her undergarments. The cold didn't bother her very much.

With a bulky fur coat in hand, she said, "Here. This should warm him up a bit." As Ed wrapped the coat around Stanley's shoulders, Kat stood on her tiptoes and ogled the teenager. She whispered, "Not bad..."

Stanley nodded and said, "Thank you."

***

Ed led Stanley to the living room. A fire crepitated in the dusty fireplace, conjuring some much needed warmth. As Stanley flumped into the sofa, Ed pushed the couch closer to the fire. He wanted the teenager to feel the warmth of the flickering flames. Like if his maternal instincts had kicked in at a moment's notice, the killer was caring for the child.

Ed glanced at the kitchen archway and asked, "You find anything for him?"

A rustling bag could be heard from the kitchen. The bag was filled with supplies and clothing scavenged from their victims.

Kat shouted, "Yeah! Give me a second!"

Ed turned towards Stanley and said, "Get yourself warmed up, boy. You don't want to freeze out here." He chuckled, then he said, "Not around us, at least."

Kat protruded her head from around the corner, simpering. Holding a pink thong with her fingertips, she asked, "Hey, sweetie, you think these will fit the boy?" Ed huffed and shook his head, Stanley nervously laughed. Kat smirked and said, "I don't know, I think they'd look good on him."

Ed smiled and said, "Stop messing around and get him something comfortable, Kat. I know you'd love to devour the boy, but he's not in the mood right now. Go on, woman, bring him something decent."

"Okay, okay... These look comfortable, though..."

Kat giggled as she returned to the kitchen. Stanley leaned forward and rubbed his hands together, trying to produce more heat. Each cool breeze wafting through the shattered windows made him shudder. He figured he'd freeze before he dried off. As he gazed at the flames, he thought about the fire sparked in his home. The constant crackling and popping sounds were oddly soothing.

Kat strolled through the archway with a simple outfit. She tossed a pair of dilapidated black sneakers on the ground – better than nothing. She threw a pair of raggedy blue jeans and a red-and-white striped long sleeve shirt on the sofa. To finish the thrifty outfit, she gently laid a red windbreaker jacket beside Stanley.

Kat placed her hands on her hips and said, "Well, there you go. It's actually not bad. I think it'll fit and it'll look good on you, hun. Now, I couldn't find any underwear in there, so you're out of luck. Well, you can always wear that thong if you want."

As Kat giggled, Stanley stared at the windbreaker jacket. The rest of the clothing was insignificant, only the vibrant red jacket caught his eye. He rubbed the garment with his fingertips, contemplating the past. *Richie's jacket,* he thought, *does she know it's his jacket?* He swallowed the lump in his throat and shook his head. Although the jacket caused a surge of bittersweet memories, he decided to shrug off his thoughts.

Under his breath, Stanley whispered, "It's nothing..."

Ed tapped Stanley's shoulder and said, "Go ahead and get dressed. I'll find you some underwear soon. Hell, I'll go buy you some if we can't find any." Stanley nodded as he slipped into his jeans. As the teenager dressed himself, Ed said, "I want you to understand something, boy. I'm proud of you. You have... *evolved* faster than most people. I mean, it takes some people decades to realize they're enslaved. It takes them a few more decades to actually free themselves. And, by the time they're free, they're as good as dead. You accomplished more at your young age than most people rotting in the ground. I'm fucking proud of you, boy."

As she leered at his lean body, Kat said, "Yeah. You're a tough, smart young man, Stanley. No matter what anyone says, you did good. They can try to make you the bad guy, but you did nothing wrong. Remember that, sweetie."

I'm proud of you – Stanley had never heard those words from his own father. He nodded, accepting the praise and advice. He smiled as he glanced down at himself. The shirt was too long and the jeans were loose. He didn't bother to try on the sneakers. From a mere glance, the shoes looked at least one size too large. He wasn't going to pose on the cover of a magazine, but at least he was clothed.

Stanley asked, "Can I... Can I stay here with you guys from now on?" He rubbed the nape of his neck, anxious. He explained, "I really don't have anywhere else to go. My family's gone, the house is gone, my best friend is gone... I don't know what I'm going to do by myself. I don't think I can survive."

Ed responded, "You're part of the family. Of course you can stay with us. I mean, shit, you can stay as long as you want. You won't be by yourself, boy."

"Really?"

"You have my word."

Kat smiled and said, "You have *our* word. We're not going to abandon you like the rest of the world. Hell, I'm definitely not going to leave you behind. We were meant to be together. Our paths were meant to collide. Some people got hurt in that crash, but we survived and we'll continue to survive together.

We're family."

Ed patted the wrinkles on Stanley's shirt, trying to iron the garment with his rough hand. Although the family resided in the woods, he wanted the boy to appear presentable. He wanted him to respect himself and his home. Regardless of clothing, though, Stanley felt more at home than ever before. He felt accepted – he finally felt *loved.*

As he gazed into the teenager's glimmering eyes, Ed said, "You're a new man with a new family. I'm proud to call you my son, Stanley."

Stanley smiled from ear-to-ear, glowing with joy. He whispered, "A new family..."

Stanley stumbled forward, wrapping his arms around Ed's body and planting his face on his chest. Ed smiled as he softly patted the boy's shoulder. Kat, feeling compelled to join, refused to be left out. Eyes swelling with tears, she embraced Ed and Stanley. The family painted a portrait of extreme violence, mental madness, and genuine love.

Chapter Fifteen

Gone Fishing

Stanley trailed Ed in the woodland, watching his 'father' with narrowed eyes. He watched the lean man, admiring each nonchalant stride. The man wore filthy brown pants, a tattered red flannel shirt, and begrimed brown boots. Yet, in the teenager's eyes, Ed shined through the filth as a charming and caring man. The only anomaly was the fishing rod slung over his shoulder.

Due to the limited supply, Stanley did not have a rod for himself. Along with his inability to play sports, he didn't know how to fish. He didn't think Ed knew how to fish, either. The pair were simply bonding. Although it was not the goal, they wouldn't complain if they could catch some fish and master the art of fishing.

Ed glanced over his shoulder and asked, "You hear that?"

Stanley stopped and tilted his head, like if the slight movement would hone his hearing. He could hear a moaning tree, a rustling bush, and a cawing bird. His eyes widened upon hearing the clashing water – *the creek.*

Stanley said, "We're close."

"You're damn right. Come on, boy, let's see what we can do with this pole."

The pair stumbled upon the local creek, which

was located only a few miles away from the abandoned house. The roaring river flowed freely, crashing on the rocks. The creek reminded Stanley of his birthday a few days prior. He reminisced about the good times. Particularly, he thought about the funnel cake and the innocent child he pummeled. The wicked thoughts became normal – he was unperturbed.

The pair shoved their pants up to their kneecaps, then they stepped into the creek. The water was refreshing and cool. Fish of all shapes and sizes swam downstream, dodging the two intruders. Stanley watched their majestic movements with a twinkle in his eye. Humanity may have abandoned him, but he could still see the beauty in nature.

Ed said, "Let's see if we can catch a bass or something out here. I'm sure I saw some... some *edible* fish last time we crossed." He wrestled with the rod, then he flung the string. The hook dangled as the line became tangled. Ed smiled and said, "If we can't catch 'em with this piece of crap, I'll do it with my bare hands."

Stanley smirked as he watched Ed's attempts at fishing – he was similarly inept at outdoor activities. He joked, "I think we're better off catching them with our hands."

"Yeah, yeah. You go ahead and try that, but I'm going to keep messing with this..."

As he stared at a large fish, Stanley asked, "How long have you been around here, Ed? I mean, how have you been surviving?"

"Shit, I've lost track. We've been around for

maybe a year or two. We've done some good and we've done some bad. To be blunt, son, we've done everything you can imagine and more to survive. And, I don't feel bad about any of it. I know Kat feels the same way."

"Were you born around here?"

"No, no. I was born out *there* somewhere. I don't remember which state. Somewhere down south, I suppose. It's a blur, but I remember bashing skulls in Texas when I was younger. I remember raping and killing in Southern California before I was eighteen. Boy, I even remember killing a few down in Mexico. Where am I from? Hell, I don't know. The moon, the ocean... I just don't know."

Stanley stared at Ed, examining his ruminative demeanor. He couldn't tell if the man was lying about his past or if he were genuinely forgetful. *The moon, the ocean,* he thought, *what is he talking about?* He tried to decipher the explanation, but to no avail. The teenager figured there was a reason for Ed's secrecy. He didn't bother to pry.

Stanley said, "If you're not from around here, if you've been all over the place, does that mean you'll leave soon?"

As the hook finally plunged into the water, Ed said, "This isn't the first abandoned house we've called home. No, we're free spirits, remember? We can live anywhere we please. So, of course we'll have to leave in a few weeks. Might even be a few days. But, don't worry about that, Stanley. You can come with us. You're not going to be left behind."

Stanley smiled, relieved. He asked, "If we leave,

where will we go? I don't think there are any more abandoned houses in the city. The other ones are filled with hobos and drug addicts. It's a little scary..."

"You don't have to be scared because it won't come to that. We're free spirits, but we don't share. If some vagrant pieces of trash refuse to move, we'll cut them up and dump them in a river. You won't have to see them. It doesn't matter, though. There are always empty houses out there. If not, we can live like hobos on our own and live happily ever after as homeless people. A tent isn't hard to come by."

"You want to live in a tent?"

"Sure. We've done it before. We can set up a little home anywhere with a tent. Shit, we can even live in someone's backyard as long as we pack before they wake. What do you think about that?"

As he stared at the fishing rod's hook in the water, Stanley shrugged and said, "It doesn't matter to me. I've never been camping before, but I'll go if you go. I just don't want to be left alone. That's all."

Ed shook his head and said, "Like I said, son, we're never going to leave you behind. No way, no how. You're too important to us. We've always wanted a child. It's just... Kat, you know, she has some issues. I think she feels better with you around. It fills a hole, you know? It fills a big, deep hole..."

Ed's ambiguous mention of Kat's 'issues' was worrisome. Issues could range from physical to mental – and everything in-between. Stanley also decided not to pry into those issues. He would let them emerge naturally. Instead, he opted to feel euphoric. Filling a gap in the couple's lives made him feel useful. For the first time since his younger years, the teenager felt like an important part of a family.

***

Standing on the protruding rocks, Stanley and Ed glanced over at the woodland behind them. To their utter surprise, a man and a young teenager emerged from the forest – a father-son duo. The pair wore matching brown waders and gray long-sleeve shirts. They carried a water cooler and a fishing rod case. From their appearance to their tools, the couple clearly meant business.

The father chuckled as he strolled towards the murderous pair. He said, "It's a nice day for fishing, isn't it? My name is Paul Lew–"

Paul stopped before he could finish introducing himself. He gazed into Ed's eyes, then he stared down at his bare feet. He glanced at Stanley with a sneer of disgust. The expression was natural for a man like himself. He was a pretentious fisherman, enjoying the activity with the most expensive equipment.

To Paul, Ed and Stanley were mere poachers, hurting the environment and the image of the activity. In his case, he was more worried about his image than the environment. The inexperienced pair gave fishermen a bad name. He didn't want to be associated with the homeless killers. He didn't want to be anywhere near them.

Paul waved and said, "Never mind, fellas. Enjoy

your day." He turned towards his son and said, "Let's head upstream, David. I think we'll catch better fish."

Stanley leaned back and examined the young teenager. *David* – the common name rang more bells than the Vatican on Christmas. He recognized the short and lean teenager. From the scruffy black hair to his dark brown eyes, he recognized David from high school. *Did he recognize me?*–Stanley thought.

As he watched the pair straggle away, Ed said, "These motherfuckers... These stupid motherfuckers. Did you see how he looked at us with those judgmental eyes? That's the way society reacts to people like us, people who have broken free from their chains. They hate us. *They despise us.* He thinks he's better than us... Don't ever believe that, Stanley. He isn't better than us. He isn't *shit* to us."

Stanley said, "I think that kid goes to my school. I've seen him on campus before. I... I don't know if he recognized me, though."

"Really? Well, that gives us more reason to teach them a lesson. They started this little confrontation, so we have to retaliate. You know what we have to do about this, right?"

"I don't..."

"We're going to finish the job. We're going to show them what the free and enlightened can accomplish. Let's do it this way: I handle the father and you handle the kid. How does that sound? What do you say to a good old father-son slaughtering?"

Stanley smiled from ear-to-ear. He said, "Okay, sure. I think I can do that."

"Good, good. Here's what we're going to do. You go talk to your little friend. Talk about homework or some bullshit like that. Then, I want you to start a fight with him. Push him, hit him, *do something.* I'm going to go hide in the woods. When this 'Paul' punk tries to break up your little fight, I'll handle him. Don't try to kill that boy until you see me, okay?"

Stanley eagerly nodded – his excitement for murder was blatant. He said, "Yeah, I understand. Can we do it now?"

Grinning, Ed gently slapped the teenager and said, "Alright, go on. You can do this, son."

***

With a jolly smile plastered on his face, Stanley approached the snobby father-son pair. He lunged on the rocks, keeping his bare feet out of the water. His mind raced with a dozen ideas – thoughts of chatter and massacre. He sought the perfect conversation starter. *What's going on at school? How's Mark doing?*

Stanley waved and said, "Hey, David. How's it going?"

David's smile was wiped off his face upon hearing Stanley's tender voice. He glanced at his classmate with a furrowed brow, then he turned towards his father. Paul shook his head and gave his son a cold shoulder. The haughty man was embarrassed of his son and his relationships.

David frowned as he turned back towards Stanley. He said, "Hey, Stanley. What are you doing here?"

Stanley said, "Not much, really. We were just trying to catch some fish."

David glanced over Stanley's shoulder – Ed had vanished. He asked, "Who was that man you were with?"

"Huh? Oh, he's just a family friend. He was trying to teach me how to fish. He's teaching me about the outdoors, you know? No big deal. So, how's it going at school? Did Mark come back yet?"

"No. I think he has to stay home now. I guess he'll be back in a few days or weeks. I don't know. Actually, where have you been? I thought I heard something about you the other day... You and your house... You live over on Manzanita, right? Wasn't there a fire around there? Was your place burned, too?"

Stanley chuckled as he rubbed the nape of his neck. He said, "No, I don't know what you're talking about. Besides, I haven't been home in a few days. I've been out here with my uncle. I'll go back home soon and we'll see if there was a fire. I–"

David interrupted, "I thought he was a family friend?"

"A family friend, an uncle, what's the difference? He's family, he's a friend. That doesn't matter to you, though. You hear me, bitch?"

David furrowed his brow and stuttered, "Wha– What? What did you say?"

"You heard me, you little faggot."

Paul glared at Stanley and sternly said, "Watch your damn mouth, boy. Don't you *ever* talk to my family like that again or I'll–"

Paul's petty threat was insignificant – a garble of noise. From his graying hair to his delicate figure, the old man posed no threat to Stanley. He could ramble on and on about what he'd do, but it did not matter. With the plan set in motion, Stanley was convinced Paul wouldn't have the opportunity to retaliate anyway. *Can a dead man fight back?*

Stanley shoved David with all of his might. David slipped, hurtling towards the ground like a falling tree – *timber!* The back of his head collided with a sturdy rock. Blood oozed from a laceration on his dome, staining the stone before the water washed it away. Paul gasped, shocked by the attack. He watched as his son convulsed in the water.

Stanley smirked and whispered, "Oops..."

Paul stuttered, "Da–David, are... are you okay? Jesus Christ..." He glared at Stanley with puffy eyes, trembling from the rage boiling within. He shouted, "What did you do?! What the hell did you do, you piece of shit?!"

As Paul rushed towards the teenager with his arms extended forward, ready to strangle him on a whim, Ed tackled the old man from behind. The pair landed safely away from the dangerous rocks. Ed punched and kicked Paul, pummeling him without mercy. Paul tried to stand, but he found himself pushed down into the water with each devastating blow.

As he beat the snobby father, Ed glanced at Stanley and said, "Finish the job. Drown that boy, Stanley."

Stanley was happy to oblige. He dragged his classmate off the rock, then planted his knees on his back. David's entire body was submerged in the creek. The blood leaking from his head stained the water like an oil spill. The teenager weakly flailed his limbs as he tried to stand, but to no avail. Water pouring into his lungs and blood gushing from his head, he couldn't escape the clutches of death.

As David's movements stopped, Stanley said, "I wish I could have done this to Mark and... and all of you."

Ed said, "Stanley, come here. I want you to see this." Ed dragged an enfeebled Paul out of the water, pulling him towards a smooth, curved rock. He glared at Paul and said, "Don't blame anyone but yourself for this. You think you can come up here and fuck with me and my boy? You think because you have a little money you can ridicule us? Mock us? You're wrong. *You're dead wrong.* Open your mouth and bite the rock, motherfucker."

Hysterically weeping, Paul stammered, "I–I–I can't... Pl–Please..."

"Bite the fucking rock! *Bite it!*"

Paul gazed at Stanley with sorrowful eyes, hoping to find some mercy. To his utter dismay, he only found a wicked soul lurking within the child. His teeth chattered as he reluctantly moved closer to the rock. He was baffled by the strange request, but he followed Ed's orders. He figured he would earn some leniency through cooperation. With a wide-open mouth, Paul's teeth scraped the curved edge of the stone.

Ed smirked and said, "Thank you, you stupid motherfucker."

Ed lifted his knee to his stomach, then he

stomped Paul's head. A grotesque sound echoed through the woodland – a loud crunch, like crackers crumbling, and an unnerving thud, like a melon falling on the kitchen floor. Stanley gasped and staggered in reverse, shocked by the savage attack. He was temporarily disoriented by the violence.

Ed curled his index finger and said, "Come here, son. Come on, don't be shy."

Stanley bit his bottom lip and approached. He trusted Ed with his life, he cherished his advice. If the man had something to show, he was going to pay attention. The grisly sight, however, made him queasy. Paul was still alive, squirming and twitching. A handful of his teeth were ejected from his mouth like pilots from falling planes. His jaw was clearly broken from the kick, too.

Ed pointed at Paul and said, "I want you to do the same. Curb stomp this bastard and show him you mean business. Do it."

Stanley inhaled deeply and nodded – *like father, like son.* He lifted his knee to his stomach and stared down at the man. Despite Paul's weak, indistinct pleas for help, Stanley stomped his head. The crunch and thud were softer on account of the missing teeth, but the damage was still severe. Blood leaked out of Paul's mouth, streaming across the stone.

Ed said, "*Again.*"

Like an obedient pup, Stanley gritted his teeth and stomped with all of his might. Paul hopped and groaned, dazed by the kick. Without another demand, Stanley continued the brutal stomping – one, two, *three kicks.* The young teenager inhaled deeply, then he stomped Paul once again. Paul was killed by the final kick.

Ed nodded and said, "Good, good... You showed initiative, you showed heart. You did a fantastic job, son. I'm proud of you."

Stanley wiped the swelling tears from his eyes, then he smiled and said, "Thank you."

"Can you drag the boy?"

"Yeah, I think so."

"Good. It's time I taught you another important lesson: when you fail to do it the right way, it's okay to do it the 'wrong' way. We didn't catch any fish, did we?"

Stanley glanced at the bloodied creek and responded, "I guess not."

"That doesn't matter. Humans are animals. Don't ever forget that. We are part of nature, whether we like it or not. When we destroy our world and disrespect this planet, it's like we're raping our own mothers. But, that's beside the point. Like animals, we don't waste anything. These bodies here will not be wasted. This old man and his son are a nutritious source of meat. I hope you're ready for a feast, son, because we're going to eat good tonight."

Stanley stared at Ed with wide eyes, astonished by the suggestion. Aside from a few of his favorite horror films, cannibalism rarely crossed his mind. Despite the horrifying suggestion, he couldn't help but smile and nod. He was happy to join his family for a special dinner, even if the meal included his former classmate.

Chapter Sixteen

Dinner

How do you prepare human flesh for consumption? The question echoed through Stanley's mind as he watched the sweltering flames in the barbecue pit. Paul's body was chopped into pieces and stuffed into black garbage bags. He didn't meet the criteria for an exquisite fine dining experience. David, on the other hand, was perfect. He was a lean young man with tender flesh – not too fat, not too muscular.

As Ed handled the finely sliced meat on the grill, Kat strolled out of the house with a stack of paper plates and a six-pack of beer. She wore a white tank top and a tiny skirt reaching down to her thighs. Her white underwear could be seen with each stride. Of course, the skimpy clothing was part of her kittenish personality. She was playfully teasing Stanley – and it worked.

Stanley salivated over his flirtatious mother-figure more than he did for the human steak. Drool streamed down his chin as he stared at her unclad legs and her swinging skirt. The boy slobbered like a dog at the dinner table, begging for a bite of the woman. Kat simpered and winked at Stanley, further aggravating his arousal.

Ed asked, "Those beers still cold?"

Kat handed the plates to Ed and said, "*Nope.* They were getting warm an hour ago. Drinking these will be like drinking piss, but some..."

"Some beer is better than none."

"That's right."

Ed and Kat shared a genuine chuckle. Stanley sat on the bench and watched the couple. Although he could not see a strong sense of intimacy, the pair shared a powerful bond – love, like a brother and sister. At the same time, he couldn't help but see a shade of his own parents. Ed was his strong and caring father while Kat was his sweet and loving mother. Of course, he felt more accepted by his new family than he did by the King family.

Ed brought Stanley a plate of charbroiled steak. The meat was unusually tantalizing, teasing his sopping taste buds. Although he knew the meat came from a human – specifically from a classmate – he couldn't help but feel starved. He had not tasted a delicious meal in days. The tender meat and succulent juices were calling his name. He could hear David's voice in his head: *Come on, Stanley, have a bite. Go ahead, eat me.*

Accepting the plate, Stanley said, "Thank you."

Ed and Kat sat beside their son, munching on the meat and slurping their beers. From their nonchalant demeanor, Stanley could see they had done this many times before. Feasting on human flesh was the norm around those woodland parts and the young teenager had to adapt. He would surely starve otherwise.

Talking with his mouth full, Ed said, "Go ahead, boy, take a bite. It's a great source of protein. That protein will help you grow big and strong. Besides, there's nothing more empowering than eating your enemies. Trust me, son, it'll make you physically and mentally stronger."

Stanley inhaled deeply, then he took his first bite. His eyes widened as the red juices squirted from between his teeth. The steak was succulent. The meat was a bit on the chewy side, but the flavor was astonishing. The human flesh made his taste buds go wild. He gnawed into the meat like a starved animal, munching and slurping.

Kat rubbed his shoulder and said, "Calm down, hun. You don't have to finish it all at once. There's plenty to go around." She took his plate and said, "Let me grab you another piece."

Stanley was happy to accept another slab of steak. He smiled and said, "Thanks."

Kat returned from the smoldering pit with a large slab of meat on Stanley's plate. Stanley took the plate and started feasting – he couldn't get enough of the meat. As the boy devoured his meal, Kat sat beside him and softly rubbed his thigh. She gently massaged his leg and ran her fingertips up to his crotch – *teasing.*

Stanley winced from the touch, like if he were about to be punched by a bully, then he nervously smiled. He gazed into Kat's glimmering eyes, lost in her wicked beauty. He thought about the peculiar situation. He thought of the woman as his 'mother' figure, but he also found her sexually attractive. Mothers, sons, and sex were never a great combination to have on the mind.

Upon spotting Kat's sexual approach, Ed huffed,

then he asked, "Why don't you two just go on and get it over with? If you're so fucking horny, just fuck each other and move on."

Staring into Stanley's eyes, Kat responded, "I'm waiting until he's ready. I don't want to spoil his first time by moving too fast. It has to be special."

Ed shook his head and said, "I was kidding, Kat. Control yourself."

As he wiped his hands on his jeans, Stanley asked, "Do... Do you really like me?"

Kat responded, "Of course, sweetie. I think I like you more than you can imagine."

"I mean... do you like-like me?"

Kat giggled from the question. The sheer innocence made her giddy. She leaned closer to Stanley, then she planted a kiss on his forehead. She pecked at the teenager's face, leaving a trail of passion. She ended up nibbling on his ear, gently kissing and sucking his earlobe. Stanley shuddered from the excitement.

Ed said, "That's enough. Stop it, Kat. Leave the boy alone."

Kat was hypnotized by her deviant lust. She licked Stanley's ear, then she moved downward. She softly planted a kiss on his neck – a loving peck. She couldn't help herself. She sucked on his neck like a pesky mosquito.

Ed sneered and yelled, "Stop it! That's enough, Kat!"

Kat leaned away from her prey and blinked erratically – the trance was broken. Stanley held the plate over his crotch, trying to hide his arousal. He stared at Ed, shocked by his outburst. He thought, *are they really a couple?*

Stanley stuttered, "I–I'm sorry if I did anything wrong..."

Ed shook his head and said, "You didn't do anything wrong, son. None of you did. It's just important that you know what you're getting into, you understand?" He sighed as he ran his fingers through his hair. He glanced at Kat and said, "If you're going to act this way, you need to let him know. Why don't you tell him *why* you like him so much? Go on, tell him about it. He needs to know everything about us. He needs to know we trust him with our deepest and *darkest* secrets, especially if you're going to act like that. *Tell him.*"

Kat said, "Okay, okay. I don't really like to tell this story, you know that, but I trust Stanley. I know he'll... he'll understand." She nervously smiled as she stared at the moist ground, preparing herself for an emotional journey. Kat said, "When... When I was younger, just a little naive girl, my brother raped me. He was probably 13 or 14 years old. About your age, sweetie. Young and handsome... He took me and he raped me. It was the most *terrifying* thing to ever happen to me. Just being grabbed and invaded like that... I still remember that feeling..."

Stanley's breathing intensified as he gazed into Kat's glimmering eyes – eyes glistening with tears. He was rattled by the story, but he couldn't conjure the courage to respond. He wanted to console the woman, but he didn't know how to comfort her.

Kat continued, "The fucked up thing is... it doesn't

bother me so much anymore. I actually *miss* that feeling. I miss my brother. Isn't that a fucked up thing to say after what happened? 'I miss the times when I was a 10 year old and my brother would rape me.' It's not right, is it? It doesn't matter, though. I guess I've been trying to capture that 'spark' ever since. I've been trying to *feel* whatever he made me feel back then..."

Stanley stared at Kat with wide eyes and a dangling jaw. The tale continued to shock him. He glanced at Ed, hoping for a punchline to a demented joke, but to no avail. Ed stared despondently at the ground, lost in his own contemplation. Stanley was at a lost for words. He sat in silence as he turned towards Kat.

Kat said, "Maybe he fucked me up or maybe I was fucked up to begin with. I really don't know. It doesn't matter anymore, does it? The past shaped me, but it's done. It can't be changed. We're here now. We're in this together and we'll stay together."

Stanley swallowed the lump in his throat, then he said, "Yeah. We're in this together. I won't leave you and I don't want you to leave me."

Kat, breaking away from her emotional character, burst into a nervous chuckle. She caressed Stanley's hair and said, "You're a sweetheart, Stanley. I won't give up on you as long as you don't give up on me. Hell, I'll even take a bullet for you."

Kat wrapped her arms around Stanley and planted a passionate kiss on his lips. Stanley was satisfied with the simple kiss. In fact, he preferred it over the nibbling of his ear and the sucking of his neck. The kiss felt genuine. He glanced over at Ed, hoping his mentor would accept the kiss and refrain from showing anger.

Ed nodded at Stanley and said, "It's fine, son. It's fine..." He chugged his beer, gulping with each swig, then he crushed the can. He said, "I think it's time for us to move on. As a family, of course. With what we've done and the damage you've caused, I'm afraid we'll be found soon. Missing kids can only stay missing for so long before the pigs get wind of the dead. It won't be long until the hounds come snooping around these woods. I know it."

Stanley despondently stared at his lap and said, "I'm sorry. I just couldn't control myself."

"There's no need to apologize. You didn't do anything wrong. You were living the way you were supposed to be living. It's the damn government and the damn laws. Still, my point stands. If they're not already looking, the entire city will be searching for us soon."

Chiming-in, Kat asked, "Well, where do you want to go? What do you have planned, Ed?"

"Nowhere specific, darling. You know that. I say we head into the city tomorrow. I want to buy some supplies with the money we've got saved up. You know, a tent, a flashlight, a hunting knife, and some boxers for the boy. We should have enough. We might be able to buy some groceries, too."

Stanley asked, "We're moving into a tent?"

Ed smiled and said, "Yeah, yeah. It's only temporary, though, so don't worry about it. The road will be our home until we find a new house. I promise you, the both of you, I'll get us a bigger house than this one. I'm going to find us a palace. We're going to get what we deserve."

Chapter Seventeen

Shopping

Ed, Kat, and Stanley strolled through the large department store, browsing each and every aisle for useful goods. Although they appeared filthy and aggressive, the group moved about in a nonchalant manner. Through the grime and scars, the trio appeared jolly. They smiled and joked, happier than the common family.

Stanley sniffled as he glanced around the store. He had visited the generic shop hundreds of times before with his real family, but he still felt like he was discovering a new world. With the knowledge he gained from Ed and Kat, the murderous teenager was seeing new colors and dimensions. He was cynical about life and humanity, but he was also much more perceptive and pensive.

As Ed and Kat walked ahead, strolling towards the outdoor area of the store, the young teenager stopped and stared down a toy aisle. A child, no older than seven years old, was sprawled on the begrimed floor, kicking and screaming. His mother stood nearby, standing with her hands on her hips and tapping her left foot. The boy threw a fit because he couldn't pick out a toy while his mother tried to play the waiting game.

Stanley scoffed and shook his head as he pondered the idea. A boy screamed at the top of his lungs for a toy while Stanley was preparing to leave society. The boy would return to a cozy home while Stanley would have to accept poverty. He wasn't bothered by his decisions, but he was amazed by the child's greed. The child didn't know better, but the fact didn't stop Stanley from judging him.

As the mother stared at him with a furrowed brow, Stanley whispered, "Beat him."

Stanley's soft whisper could not be heard from down the aisle, especially with the child's screaming, but he hoped the woman could read his lips. Although he did not have experience as a parent, he figured his simple advice was valuable. *Beat him and he'll stop crying, beat him and he'll learn the value of life.*

As the woman tilted her head and gazed at him, Stanley waved and walked away. His red windbreaker jacket whooshed with each step. He simpered as he approached Ed and Kat. The couple stood near a large camping tent display, carefully examining the equipment and the price tags.

Ed's blood-red flannel shirt and thick beard stood out like a sore thumb. Kat, on the other hand, wore a faded blue sundress. A black tote bag dangled from her shoulder, obviously belonging to a victim of the past. Although she had her fair share of scars, Stanley found more beauty than terror in her soul.

As the teenager approached, Ed asked, "What do you think? You like it?"

Stanley turned his attention to the display. He didn't really have to think about his opinion. The answer was always going to be 'yes.' He simply wanted to humor his mentor. He wanted to make the conversation a bit more lively. The tent could be five-by-five feet and he would still feel more free than when he slept in his own home.

Stanley said, "I think it's perfect for us."

Kat responded, "Great. Go ahead and pick the color, sweetie. I want to know your favorite."

"I want the blue and gray one. Blue is my favorite color. It reminds me of the sky. It makes me feel free, I guess..."

Ed lifted a large white box from beside the display. He said, "Alright. We'll just grab some flashlights, then we'll be on our way. I don't think I'll be able to buy a knife around here, not with all of these eyes watching us. These 'consumer' knives are shit anyway. Come on."

Kat pointed at an aisle to the right. She said, "I'll be right back. I have to pick something up."

With eager eyes, Stanley asked, "What? What is it?"

"Well, I can't tell you since it's a little secret. Just stay with Ed, I'll be right back."

Kat giggled as she walked towards the aisle at the back of the store. She browsed the products cluttered on the shelves – tampons, pregnancy tests, warming jelly and the like. Her eyes widened upon spotting the condoms. She shoved a black box of regular-size condoms into her bag, then she strolled away. She couldn't help but giggle as her imagination ran wild. Kat and Stanley were nearing a big step in their relationship and Kat was ready to leap forward.

As Kat approached the pair, Ed asked, "What's got you so happy, girl?"

Kat shrugged and said, "Nothing, nothing..."

"Yeah, yeah. You better not be up to anything that will get us busted. You know better than that, right? *Right?*"

"Of course. It's nothing, Ed. Really, it's something for me and Stanley, if you know what I mean..."

Ed rolled his eyes and marched forward. He said, "Alright, I get you. Come on, let's start heading out. You've got the money, right?"

"Yeah. Should be enough for everything."

The family of murderers approached the foyer of the store. As expected, only two cash registers were open and the cashiers were working at a snail's pace. Minimum wage promoted minimum effort for some employees. The lines were brimming with people eager to checkout and rush home.

Ed sighed, then he said, "Let's just hurry up and get in line. I don't want to waste anymore time with these people."

Stanley reluctantly followed the couple. He loved Ed and Kat with all of his heart, but the monotony of waiting in line was never welcoming. The enigmatic couple could not enliven the tedium of a twenty-minute wait. To his left, he could see the bustling electronics section. He had flashbacks to the days he visited the store with his mother and brother. Only a few days ago, he convinced his mother to allow him to visit the electronics section while she waited in line – he decided to do the same with his new parents.

Stanley tugged on Kat's dress and asked, "Can I go look at the video games before we leave? Please?"

Kat smiled as she gazed into Stanley's innocent eyes, then she glanced at Ed. She wasn't the leader of the family, so she sought permission before approving. Ed bit his bottom lip and nodded – *let him go.*

Kat said, "Go on. Have some fun. Try to be back in ten minutes, okay? Don't talk to anyone, either. You never know what kind of people shop in these kind of stores..."

Stanley jogged towards the other side of the store, slipping and sliding between the slothful customers. He slowed his jog to a leisurely stroll as he approached the electronics section. His eyes widened as he examined the shelves of video games, which were located behind sturdy glass.

He stopped in front of a handheld gaming system; the demo, of course, was latched onto a sturdy stand to prevent theft. He played as a plumber wearing denim overalls and a red cap, jumping on anything and everything in his path.

Stanley whispered, "I'm going to miss this..."

The young teenager lived a sheltered life for fourteen years. He was young, so he didn't have to experience the real world yet. The plunge made him nervous. He couldn't help but wonder how he would live without technology. Only the freedom of the open road waited for him ahead – no more video games or internet. He was taking a step back from technology while taking one giant step forward in his life.

With bittersweet thoughts running through his mind, Stanley whispered, "It's going to get better. All of us will be happy together. I don't need this. I don't need any of this."

An elderly woman watched Stanley with narrowed eyes from afar, astonished. She rubbed her eyes and shook her head, like if she were trying to awaken from a dream, but to no avail. To the untrained eye, he seemed like any other boy playing a video game. The woman, however, recognized him. She had seen him on the news, she heard about him on the radio, and she read about him in the paper. Stanley was a living headline to her.

As she held her trembling hand to her quivering lips, the woman whispered, "It's him... Jesus, it's him..." She scurried towards an employee and whispered, "It's the boy from the news. It's actually him."

***

Ed and Kat slowly moved forward, walking two steps for every paid customer. The couple were practically crawling towards the finish line, shambling like the undead in a horror movie. A few arrogant patrons sneered at the pair, scoffing at their lack of hygiene. Yet, the couple didn't seem to care. They only sought to escape civilization.

Ed clenched his jaw and tilted his head as he neared the cash register – only three customers remained until they reached the finish line. The excitement of finally departing did not unnerve him, though. A simple newspaper sitting on a rack caught his attention. From afar, he swore the image on the front page depicted a younger Stanley. The fact irked him, sending him into a tailspin of uncertainty.

Ed placed the hefty box on the ground, then he trudged out of the line. Kat watched him with a furrowed brow, baffled by his behavior. With each calculated step, Ed slowly approached the rack. The jitters increased as his view became clearer. The front page headline read: *Family killed in suspicious fire, son sought for questioning.*

Ed was not illiterate, but he had some trouble reading. Despite his disability, he was able to skim through the article. He found several mentions of Stanley's name and the word 'suspicious.' Considering Stanley's heinous actions, 'suspicious' did not sit well with him. Ed winced as Kat gently tapped his shoulder.

Kat asked, "What's wrong?"

Ed stared at Kat with sharp eyes. He said, "They... They know..." He showed Kat the newspaper, tapping the image of Stanley – an old middle school picture. Ed repeated, "*They know.*"

Kat slowly shook her head and said, "No, no... I'm not going to let him go. It's not happening, Ed, not now."

"Keep your voice down. I know that already. If we want to keep him, if we want to *save* him, we have to get out of here as soon as possible."

Ed and Kat rushed towards the electronics section, leaving their supplies behind. A few customers in line called to the couple, complaining about the heavy tent and flashlights rolling on the floor, but the pair refused to stop. They had their sights set on saving Stanley from the prying customers and under-trained security officers.

Ed smiled as he turned the corner and spotted Stanley. The teenager stood near the handheld system, enjoying the game demo. The smile on his face caused a swarm of butterflies to dance in his stomach. In his mind, the boy was part of his bloodline. Kat did not birth him, but he was their son and his happiness was significant.

The savage killer's smile was wiped from his face as a loss prevention officer approached from the other side of the aisle. The frail elderly woman followed closely behind, pointing and whispering. The man was burly, his navy polo shirt clung to his muscles with each stride. Appearance didn't represent strength, but Ed would certainly be facing a challenge if the pair bumped heads.

Ed ran forward and shouted, "Stanley! Stanley, come here, boy!"

Stanley glanced at his mentor with a furrowed brow. He glanced towards his left and gasped upon spotting the security personnel. Before he could utter a word, Ed carried him away from the demo.

In a sonorous tone, the security officer shouted, "Stop! Sir, stop!"

Ed disregarded the demands and ran away. He grabbed Kat's forearm and yanked her towards him. He glanced towards the entrance to his left, then he sprinted towards his right. To his utter dismay, two police officers had already arrived at the scene. Ed stopped behind an aisle and dropped Stanley. Stanley landed on his feet, startled by the experience. The world was moving quicker than ever before.

Out of breath, Ed said, "Whatever happens... I want you to run. You understand me? Don't... Don't stop for anyone. Just keep running." He placed his hand on Kat's cheek and gazed into her eyes. He said, "We've been through a lot, sweetheart. If it comes down to it, I want you to run away with the boy. Forget about me."

Kat sniveled and moaned. She said, "I don't want it to end like this..."

Upon hearing the rapid footsteps in the neighboring aisle, Ed said, "We have to go."

Stanley opened his mouth to speak, wanting to chime-in and spill his heart, but he was forced to run. Ed led the way, running ahead as he frantically searched for the best exit. Kat trailed the leader of the family, opting to stay closer to Stanley. She refused to lose the teenager in the chaos. The trio slipped into a home appliance section, crouching beneath the washing and drying machines.

Ed whispered, "Kat, go up ahead with the boy."

With a quivering lip, Kat asked, "What are you going to do? Huh? What the hell are you planning, Ed?" Ed bit his bottom lip and shook his head. Kat said, "Don't pull any of this macho bullshit now, asshole. Don't do this to us. Let's leave together. Let's be a family and–"

"Not yet. I have to take one with me. Go on ahead. I'll be right there."

Stanley said, "I'll help you. I can–"

"*Go.*"

Kat whimpered as she stared at her partner in crime. She was irked by his foolish decision, but she didn't bother to challenge him. He was a free spirit, he followed his own rules. Stanley was astonished by his strict rejection. He couldn't challenge him, either. He wouldn't disrespect his mentor during such an unfortunate time. The pair reluctantly straggled away, crawling towards the other end of the aisle.

Ed planted his back on a drying machine and stared at the ceiling. He pulled out his trusty serrated blade as he counted the passing seconds. The sound of boots thudding on the tile flooring increased as someone approached. Ed inhaled deeply, then he lunged at his pursuer. He found himself confronting a police officer.

The officer was startled by Ed's sudden appearance. The hesitant cop drew his handgun, quickly firing one round. To his disappointment, the gunshot missed the killer's torso by an inch. Ed pushed the officer's gun away before he could fire another shot, then he stabbed the man's throat. The officer dropped the gun, grabbing Ed's forearm with his right hand and trying to cover his wound with the other.

The cop's attempts were rendered fruitless as Ed twisted the blade. Blood squirted on the killer's face as the officer grunted and groaned. Like a waterfall, blood poured from the officer's mouth and streamed down his chin. He was brutalized in an instant.

Through his clenched jaw, Ed said, "You stupid motherfuckers think you can change us. You think you can come into our lives and rape our souls. You were wrong about that. You were dead wrong, you son of a bitch."

Ed yanked the knife out of the officer's throat, then he shoved him away. The man was enfeebled by the stabbing, plummeting to the floor like a bomb at war. Ed glanced around the store. The loud gunfire caused the customers to scatter like cockroaches shocked by a blinding light. As he glared at the officer, fueled by an irrepressible hatred for authority, Ed picked up the handgun.

He pushed the officer's arms aside, then he sat on his chest. He shoved the barrel of the handgun into the wound on the officer's neck, further aggravating the grisly laceration. The cop squirmed and wheezed as he struggled to escape. Ed twisted the handgun in the wound, aiming upward towards the cop's head, then he pulled the trigger. Unlike the officer, he did not hesitate to kill.

As he stared at the streak of blood and brains on the floor, Ed whispered, "Good night and sweet dreams, motherfucker..."

Ed glanced towards his right as a barrage of footsteps approached. The department store's loss prevention officers rushed towards the thunderous gunfire. They were shocked to find the police officer sprawled atop a pool of blood. Ed smirked as the employees staggered in reverse with their hands up – *terrified*.

Ed waved at the employees, then he jogged down the aisle. Their respect and obedience allowed them to survive. Although he despised authority, he didn't mind stroking his ego through power. Ed gritted his teeth as he spotted Kat and Stanley lingering near the exit.

Ed asked, "What the hell are you doing? I told you to go, I told you to run. What are you still doing here?!"

Stanley responded, "I don't want to run. You said you wouldn't leave me behind, so I'm not leaving you behind. We're supposed to be family, remember?"

Teary-eyed, Kat rubbed Stanley's shoulder and said, "He's right. We weren't going to leave. We wouldn't survive without you. Fuck that, I'd rather die than break our family apart."

Ed tapped his brow with the bloodied barrel of the gun as he shook his head. He murmured, "You stupid motherfuckers..." Despite his disappointment, he couldn't help but smile. His family was strong and he was proud of them. He said, "Fuck it. Let's get the hell out of here."

With a dead police officer left in their wake, the family exited the store.

Chapter Eighteen

A Chase

Ed, Kat, and Stanley jostled through the inquisitive crowd. (Although the customers heard gunfire and frantic shouting, they couldn't help but wait and watch – r*ubbernecking.*) In the foyer of the store, police officers barked their demands and called for help. Of course, the absconding group did not comply.

As he stumbled out of the crowd, Ed glanced around the parking lot. The dazzling sun partially blinded him, but he could see his selection of getaway vehicles. The parked cars, however, were out of the question. He wasn't going to spend time trying to hot-wire a car – it would be foolish. Fortunately, a young woman sat in her cherry-red sedan nearby, watching the commotion.

Ed glanced over his shoulder, staring at Kat and Stanley. He said, "Stick together and follow me."

Cars swerved and blared their horns as the family sprinted through the parking lot. The nosy woman's eyes widened upon spotting Ed. She couldn't have known Ed was responsible for the chaos inside of the store, but his mere appearance struck fear into her heart. She turned and tried to lock her door, but to no avail.

Ed pulled the driver's door open and yelled, "Get out! Leave the keys and get out of the damn car!"

The woman held her hands up and indistinctly yammered as she gazed into Ed's bestial eyes. The killer tapped the barrel of the handgun on the woman's face and shouted, "Get out of the car, damn it! *Get out!*"

The woman was paralyzed by her fear. Ed grabbed a fistful of her blonde hair, then he yanked her out of the car. She wept and screamed from the pain. Ed shoved the woman to the ground, then he glanced around the steering wheel. To his delight, the keys were still in the ignition.

Ed said, "Get in here. Hurry your asses up!"

Ed sat in the driver's seat, Kat took the passenger's seat, and Stanley hopped into the back seat. The wheels squealed as Ed sped out of the parking lot. The sedan jounced with each speed bump, causing the trio to sway every which way. The family could see the cops rushing out of the department store and the customers pointing at their car. The emergency sirens wailing beyond the horizon were equally disquieting.

As he took a sharp right and exited the parking lot, Ed shouted, "Get your seat belts on! This is going to be one hell of a ride!"

Ed glanced at the rear view mirror as he stomped on the gas pedal. He could see the cars rolling to the side of the road, making way for the convoy of police cruisers – a dozen, at least. The police were rapidly approaching, hurtling towards the sedan. The vibrant red color of the car made them an easy target to track, too.

Fearless and careless, Ed swerved into the

oncoming lane. Kat pressed her left hand on the ceiling of the car and her other hand on the dashboard, trying to keep her balance. Stanley buried his face in his knees, blocking out the madness. He could still hear Ed's husky breathing and indistinct whispers above the blaring horns and sirens.

The oncoming vehicles barely evaded the red sedan, swerving into other lanes and stomping on their brakes. The daring move did not dissuade the police, though. One police cruiser followed directly behind the sedan while the rest of the convoy trailed the car from the right lane. The police were certainly persistent.

As he spotted the pursuing car, Ed punched the steering wheel and shouted, "Damn it! Damn it!" His eyes widened upon spotting an escape route. He glanced at Kat and Stanley, then he said, "Hold on. Just hold on..."

Ed took another sharp turn into an alley. With the pedal to the metal, he hurtled down the alleyway. Ed and Kat gasped as a homeless man shambled towards the center of the narrow path. The man, wrapped in layers of tattered coats, staggered upon spotting the zooming vehicle. His fight-or-flight response told him to wait and see – *maybe it'll stop in time, maybe it'll just disappear.*

The speeding sedan charged through the man at a breakneck speed – likely breaking the man's neck. The homeless man was tossed four meters into the air, vaulting over the car. As he glanced over his shoulder, Ed caught a glimpse of the man spiraling towards the ground. Even over the roaring engines and wailing sirens, the thud of a living person hitting pavement echoed into the sedan.

Ed took a sharp left and found himself barreling into a busy street. Dozing in-and-out of consciousness, the oblivious drivers waiting for the light were in for a rude awakening.

As he slowed the car, dropping from 70 to 30 miles per hour, Ed said, "Take the wheel, Kat."

Wide-eyed, Kat repeated in a dubious tone, "Take the wheel?"

"Take the damn wheel!"

Kat reluctantly leaned over the driver's seat and carefully handled the steering wheel. Ed rolled his window down, then he protruded his head from the opening. With one eye closed and the other squinted, the murderer aimed the handgun towards the alley. His breathing was controlled, his demeanor was composed.

With the wind blowing through his hair, he fired three rounds at the pursuing police cruiser. The bullets penetrated the windshield, hitting the driver twice in the chest. The black-and-white car swerved as the police officer lost control. At a high speed, the car crashed into a parked truck. The sound of shattering glass and clanking metal reverberated through the street.

Ed smiled as several police cruisers pulled over near the crash site while others slowed their pursuit. The cops weren't going to have a shootout on a busy street, especially without the proper preparations. Ed glanced over at the road ahead. His eyes widened as the car cruised towards a busy intersection. He slipped back into the car, shoving Kat aside. He stomped on the brakes and veered to the right. The car bounced over a stone divider, then they crashed into the back of a black van.

***

With his face planted on the steering wheel, Ed muttered, "Shit... Shit... We fucked up." He leaned back in his seat and sniffled as blood oozed from his nostrils. Ed said, "We're cornered... We really fucked up this time. Damn it."

Kat groaned as she lifted her head from the dashboard. She had a grisly laceration on the left side of her forehead. Stanley, on the other hand, emerged unscathed. His body ached and he was mentally scarred, but he was not severely injured. The seat belt saved him.

With a quivering lip, Stanley asked, "Wha–What are we going to do now? What's... What's going to happen to us?"

Ed stared at the van ahead. A mother, a father, and two little girls scampered out of the vehicle. He glanced at the rear-view mirror, then at the side-view mirrors. Traffic was brought to a halt by the collision and the surrounding police officers. Drivers were being removed from their vehicles and cops positioned themselves in several vantage points.

Ed licked his lips, then he said, "Well, son, this is the end for me. They don't take kindly to cop killers. I'm not too sure about you, but I hope you find a way out of all of this. You're a bright kid, so I think you'll be okay. Just try not to worry about it, okay? Don't worry..."

Teary-eyed, Ed leaned out of the window. He gritted his teeth and grunted as he fired five rounds at a tree across the street. He knew an officer was hiding behind the tree, waiting for the perfect opportunity to strike. The savage serial killer wouldn't allow it. He created his life's path, so he chose the time of his death. Before he could empty the clip, a bullet tore through his left shoulder.

Ed shouted, "Damn it! Damn it!" As Kat and Stanley leaned towards him to offer aid and support, the man scowled and shook his head. With thick veins bulging on his neck and brow, Ed said, "It's too late. Get down... Get down and take cover."

As she sniffled, Kat asked, "What? What are you saying?"

Ed loudly sighed, then he said, "They're going to shoot us up like a bunch of animals. Take cover..."

Kat trembled in her seat, astonished. The fear of death crept up on her like never before. Ed grunted and groaned as he climbed into the back seat. Through the excruciating pain, he smiled and wrapped his arms around Stanley. He pushed Stanley down towards the seat, covering the teenager's body with his own.

Before Stanley could utter a single word, an orchestra of thunderous gunshots erupted. The deafening gunfire was accompanied by the sounds of shattering glass and splintering metal. Dozens of bullets penetrated the sedan, tearing through Ed and Kat like paper. The surrounding officers were shooting to kill.

As he protected Stanley from the hail of bullets, Ed weakly said, "I... I love you, son. I love you."

Fifteen seconds of gunfire felt like fifteen minutes. As the crepitations dwindled, Stanley opened his eyes and gasped. With his back on the seat, the teenager gazed into Ed's hollow eyes. His mentor's body rested on top of him, stiff and lifeless. The vicious head of the family was slain by a barrage of bullets – killed while protecting his child.

Stanley inhaled deeply as he used all of his strength to slide out from underneath Ed. He examined Ed from head-to-toe. He was rattled as he gazed into his eyes – eyes devoid of life. His father figure, the man he learned to love, had bloodied craters scattered across his torso and arms. In a final attempt to save his son, Ed became a human shield.

Kat wheezed and squirmed in the passenger seat, writhing in anguish. She grimaced and wept as she held her stomach. Without moving her hand, she could see her dress was stained with blood. She glanced towards her left shoulder and shuddered. She didn't realize she was also shot in the shoulder – it was numb.

Kat said, "Ed... Ed, what do we do?"

Stanley continued to stare into Ed's eyes, hoping he would awaken and respond. The dead, however, could not speak. Reanimation was impossible. Hope was nonexistent.

As she caught a glimpse of Ed's condition through the rear-view mirror, Kat said, "No... No, no, no. Not you, Ed, not you..."

Kat mewled like a newborn baby, whimpering

and shivering. Tears streamed down her cheeks and plopped onto her bag. The pain, emotional and physical, was too much to endure. As her bottom lip quivered, she opened her bag and stared down into it. Never in her life did she imagine a box of condoms would bring such a bittersweet feeling to her body.

With a nervous smile, Kat glanced back at Stanley and said, "I want you to wait here, sweetie. You sit here and wait until it's over." She grimaced as she grabbed the handgun from the floorboard. As she opened the door, Kat said, "You're a special one, hun. I'll always love you."

As the door closed behind the woman he adored, Stanley whispered, "Wait..."

Kat staggered towards the center of the street with the handgun hidden under her dress. She teetered towards a roadblock, laughing deliriously. The surrounding officers barked their demands, trying to defuse the situation before it could erupt. The woman, however, was set to self-destruct.

Kat muttered, "I won't... I won't let you take him... You can't touch him, you can't have him... He's... He's not like you." She stopped fifteen meters away from the roadblock. She inhaled deeply, then she shouted, "I won't let you touch him! *I love him!*"

Kat scowled as she lifted the firearm and aimed at the roadblock. Before she could pull the trigger, police officers riddled her with a volley of blistering bullets. Her body convulsed from the gunfire spewing out of the armory of handguns and rifles. As the gunfire stopped, the vicious woman staggered to her knees, then she fell to her side.

Through the broken rear window in the sedan, Stanley watched the showdown. He watched as Kat was gunned down like a sick animal with a contagious disease, hit with dozens of bullets from every corner. He knew she had mental issues, but he didn't think she was sick. He wondered if her public execution was justified. He pondered what he could do to avenge her.

Reading his thoughts out loud, Stanley said, "Nothing... I can't do anything to avenge you, Kat. I'm sorry."

Chapter Nineteen

Consequences

Stanley sat in the back seat of a police cruiser. His face and hands were wiped clean, but his clothing was already stained with Ed's blood. A bit of Richie's blood was smeared around the stabbing holes, too, but he didn't care to think about him. His deceased best friend was a remnant of the past, a reminder of another life.

Instead, Stanley sat and pondered his current situation, contemplating the potential consequences of his actions. A teenage killer could not be punished to the fullest extent of the law. Lethal injection was the least of his concerns. He thought about spending a lifetime in jail, forced back into his restraints. He thought about his fellow prisoners, fearing he would be subjected to endless rape.

Stanley whispered, "I didn't do it... No, I didn't do it. It wasn't me, *it was them*. It was all their idea." He spoke as if he were trying to convince himself of a fallacy. He repeated, "I didn't do it, I didn't do it..."

Stanley glanced to his left as the door swung open. A dark-haired man stood before him. The man was not like the other police officers – not in appearance or demeanor. He donned a black leather jacket over a white button-up shirt. His black pleated trousers matched his polished dress shoes. His short black hair complemented his stubble. He was a simple man.

The man said, "Hello, son. I'm Detective Jeremy Anderson. You can call me 'Jeremy.' Don't worry about the formalities. No need for 'sir' or 'mister.' You're not in school or anything like that. Okay? So, what's your name, kiddo?"

Stanley swallowed the lump in his throat, then he said, "My name is Stanley. Stanley King."

"It's nice to meet you, Stanley. Listen, I have some questions for you and I hope you cooperate. I want you to know, I'm only trying to help. If you feel uncomfortable, let me know and I'll see what I can do for you. You don't have to answer anything you don't want to. But, I'm really going to need your help, alright? You help me and I'll help you. That's how it works."

"Okay."

"Great. Did you know the couple in the vehicle?"

Stanley glanced at the bullet-riddled sedan as he pondered his response. He wanted to admit to the help Ed offered him. He wanted to spill his heart and confess his deep love for Kat. Yet, he knew the detective wouldn't understand. He had to play a game if he wanted to survive. Wasting time thinking about his answer didn't help, so he decided to tackle the problem head-on.

Stanley said, "No. They took me from my home and they... they kept me hostage."

Anderson bit his bottom lip and nodded. He said, "Okay. Was this before or after the fire at your house?"

"*After.* They burned the house down and then they

took me with them. They said they always wanted a kid like me. So, they took me."

"Do you know what happened to your parents and your brother, Stanley? Are you fully aware of the incident?"

"They killed them, right? They killed my mom, my dad, and my brother, then they... they burned the house down."

"Yeah, I suppose that theory could work... I wouldn't be here asking you questions if your guardians weren't deceased. I'm truly sorry about that, too," Anderson said as he despondently stared at the wicked child. "Now, where did they take you after the fire? We've been looking for you for quite some time, son. I'd really like to know where these people were hiding you."

Stanley opened his mouth to speak, but he stopped himself before he could utter a sound. He needed a moment to think about his time at the abandoned house – a moment to consider the evidence he might have left behind. He didn't spend much time at the house, but he was positive the police would be able to find a speck of his DNA – somewhere, somehow.

Stanley said, "I don't know. They took me to an abandoned house and they kept me locked in a room. They blindfolded me when I went there and when I left."

Anderson furrowed his brow and asked, "Are you sure about that, son?"

Stanley rapidly nodded and said, "I'm positive."

"*Okay.* So, what were you doing out here today?

What did they tell you? I've read some reports, I've seen some footage, and you didn't seem too scared out here today. You understand what I'm saying? You seemed normal. Now, if they kidnapped you and hurt your family, why didn't you ask anyone for help?"

"Because... Because they were going to hurt me if I screamed. So, I... I was going to wait until I saw a cop, then I was going to ask for help. There weren't a lot police officers around, though, so I just stayed quiet. I didn't want anything bad to happen."

Anderson smiled and nodded, like if he were accepting the teenager's explanation – or accepting his challenge. He said, "Okay, okay. I have a few more questions for you, so please bear with me. I'll have you out of here soon, though. Don't worry about that. I just need to know about... Let's see... Tell me about Richie Adams. You remember your classmate, right? What happened to him?"

Stanley narrowed his eyes and responded, "You should tell me. I don't know. Did something happen to him? Did something happen to Richie?"

"I think we'll find out soon, Stanley. We'll also be talking about your trip to *Adventure Planet*. But, I think we'll continue our chat later. Thank you for your cooperation, young man. I'll have an officer bring you some water, then we'll take you downtown. Sit tight."

Stanley sat in silence as the detective closed the door, brooding. He couldn't help but wonder if his ruse worked. He felt a sense of remorse for pinning his crimes on Ed and Kat, but he still felt nothing for his best friend and his family. The slaughtered were merely used as puppets to convince the public of a heinous crime. *I'm the victim,* Stanley thought, *it can work, they have to believe me.*

Anderson walked away from the back seat. He moseyed towards an everyday beat cop. The blue-eyed officer with blonde hair leaned on the front of the car, nonchalantly sipping coffee from a paperboard cup. An embroidered name tag on his chest read: *V. Cook.*

Anderson stood near the officer and said, "Such a tragic day, isn't it?" Cook sighed and nodded as he stared at the massacre. Anderson said, "We'll get to the bottom of this. These people... These *savages* won't get away with this."

Cook sniffled, then he asked, "What did you think about the boy? You think he was abducted or tricked, or something like that?"

"The boy? Well, to be blunt with you, officer, I think the boy is a damn liar. From the second he started speaking, I could tell he was one of them. Now, it might be difficult to prove, but I know I can break him. I know he had something to do with the fire, he was involved with his friend's disappearance, and he was involved in that attack at the park. He's one of them. You can see it in his eyes. He's a feral animal acting like a domesticated pet."

Cook furrowed his brow and asked, "Are you sure about that?"

"*I'm positive.* Listen, when you head down to the station, I want you to take special care of his clothing. You understand me? Hand it over to forensics as soon as possible. I think he might be wearing the clothing of a victim – maybe even a few. Don't let him know why, though, just make sure he doesn't try to ruin any of it. It's going to be *very* important for the case."

"Yeah, okay."

Anderson patted Cook's shoulder and nodded – a nonverbal 'thank you' and 'goodbye.' As the detective strolled towards his unmarked car, Cook glanced over his shoulder and peered into the back seat of his cruiser. Through the cage partition, he could see Stanley sitting in the back seat. The officer shuddered upon spotting the bestial look in his eyes. A spark of deviance lingered in the windows to his soul. The boy was not human. He was a vessel for a beast of unfathomable horrors...

Join the Mailing List

Stanley and his family of violence would surely appreciate it if you signed up for my mailing list. That's not a threat, though, it's just a *recommendation.* You'd be the first to know about free books, deep discounts, and new releases. You'll only receive one or two emails a month, too, so you don't have to worry about spam. Best of all, it requires little effort on your part. Click here to sign-up: http://eepurl.com/bNl1CP

Dear Reader,

First and foremost, thank you for reading! I'm glad you finished the book. If you didn't finish it and you'd like to hurl some hurtful messages at me, you can find my Twitter and Facebook links at the end of this segment. Anyway, your readership is truly invaluable to me. *A Family of Violence* was fueled by my love for dark fiction and storytelling – much like the rest of my horror books. I pride myself in delivering uncompromising stories, delving into taboo territory with little shame. At the same time, I never intend on offending or appalling anyone. If any of the content in this book truly offended you, please accept my sincerest apologies.

A Family of Violence wasn't inspired by a particular novel or film. It wasn't inspired by a real incident, either. The idea came from a lifetime of horror and my education in criminology. There are many pieces of media out there about serial killers. Many of these terrifying works, however, tend to stay away from child murderers – by that I mean, *children that kill.* It's a horrifying subject and it really captured my attention. Of course, it also fits with the theme of nature vs. nurture. Are people born evil or is it taught to them? I didn't delve too deeply into the theme with Stanley, though.

Edward and Katina fit a more traditional mold – something that's easier to grasp. This enigmatic couple kill people without a shred of remorse. They also fit the nature vs. nurture theme. On one hand, Edward has been killing for as long as he could remember. He is naturally evil. Katina, on the other hand, reached a breaking point during her appalling experience with her brother. So, her breed of evil was wired at a later time. And, her evil was fostered by her relationship with Edward.

In terms of criminology, I also tossed in a bit of the Macdonald triad in *A Family of Violence*. For those who don't know, the triad links animal cruelty, fire setting and bed-wetting to violent behavior. Early in the book, Stanley suggests the killing of a squirrel. He also persistently wets the bed and he plays with fire. It's an interesting concept – a *fascinating* concept, really. I'm rambling, though. I'm sure you can spot the other tidbits spread throughout the book.

Anyway, if you enjoyed this book, *please* leave an honest review on Amazon.com. Your review is incredibly significant. In fact, my career *depends* on your review. Your review will help me improve on future books and it will help other readers find this book. The more readers I garner, the more I can write. So, if you liked this book, a review will help me release more. It will also allow me to gauge interest for certain genres and themes. Do you like dark serial killer novels? Did this book go 'too far?' Would you like to go further into the dark mind? Your review has the power to influence my writing – please use it wisely.

Also, feel free to share this book with your friends and family. Tweet it to your followers on Twitter, share it with your friends and family on Facebook, lend it to them, or even read it to them over the phone or video chat. Birthday, holiday, or special event coming up? Buy them a copy as a gift. Word-of-mouth is a superb method in supporting independent authors – and it's mostly *free.* My life consists of cheap noodles and tap water. I occasionally watch a movie or two on VHS. I need your support to sustain this 'thrifty' lifestyle.

Finally, if you enjoy scary stories, feel free to visit my Amazon's author page. I've published over a *dozen* horror anthologies and several novels. Like slasher horror books? Check out my gory slasher, *Butcher Road.* It's inspired by classic horror films and other notorious serial killers. Looking for a violent thriller? I recommend reading *Captives and Captors.* This mystery-thriller adds a dash of extreme horror to create an unnerving experience. Furthermore, many of my books are available on Kindle Unlimited! I publish books frequently, so please keep your eyes peeled for the next release. I'm currently working on my first science-fiction/fantasy book and another serial killer novel. Once again, thank you for reading. Your readership keeps me going through the darkest times!

Until our next venture into the dark and disturbing,

Jon Athan

P.S. If you have questions (or insults), you'll receive the quickest and most efficient response via Twitter @Jonny_Athan. If you're an aspiring author, I'm always happy to lend a helping hand. I know how difficult it can be to get started, so feel free to ask. You can also *like* my Facebook page and talk to me there. Thanks again!

Made in the USA
Monee, IL
03 August 2023

40437094R00114